IC

A ⌐ THE

DEPTON SHADELINGS

J A BOWLER

Dedicated to Ayla, who also prefers animals.

Contents

Chapter 1
Depton

It had been raining continuously for two weeks and water had soaked through every pore of the Earth, until it could hold no more, leaving it brimming over like a weeping child. Ice Cooper peered with difficulty through the windscreen. The wipers were failing dismally to deal with the glutinous sheets which cascaded down the glass surface. Her father was having to concentrate hard on the road conditions; he was driving slowly, keeping the engine revs high and leaning forward as if looking more closely through the murk would help. It didn't.

A man was unexpectedly in the middle of the road. Ice's father pressed hard on the horn and jammed his foot on the brakes, locking up the wheels and causing the car to glide in a skidding arc over the wet surface; the vehicle lurched to a stop and stalled, sending her nine-year-old brother's mobile phone shooting out of his hand into the foot-well. It was amazing that her father had managed to miss hitting the man who now stood by the driver's window and stared in at them.

"What are you doing?" Ice's father shouted, winding down the window in fury. He wanted to swear, Ice knew, but he was suppressing it in front of her and Oscar. Buddy, the rescue boxer dog who had been asleep next to Oscar on the back seat, shot up and true to his kind, gave a gruff bark and 'punched' the window, making a wet, muzzle-shaped smear. From the passenger seat, Ice peered over at the strange person, trying to work out why he had stepped without caution, into the path of the traffic on Depton High Street. She felt a jolt of alarm as the man, slack-jawed and wide-eyed, met her gaze. He was wearing a drenched, padded green jacket which no longer offered him any protection against the rain. The hood hung limply down the back and the grey, fake fur which rimmed it, was now a sodden fringe. Ice could see that the front of the coat was covered with all manner of plastic badges – cartoon animals, political slogans, rock bands...

"They're here," the man wailed into the open window, "look!" He was pressing the knuckles of one fist to his mouth, like a small, frightened child, and with the other hand, was pointing frantically up the street. As Ice turned to look, the man skirted abruptly round the bonnet of the car and disappeared into a side road. Her father, stunned, watched him go and then gathered his wits sufficiently to restart the engine.

"I hope that's not an omen," he said, laughing sheepishly as he put the car into gear. "Do you think they're all mad in Depton?" He looked back at the two children and pulled one of those wry faces that people do when they want to make light of something that is both odd and troubling. Oscar emerged from scrabbling for his phone and sniggered.

"Hello. I'm from a 1970s sci-fi movie!" he said, putting on a fake American Hollywood accent. Ice glanced over at him, sneering slightly. Her brother was something of a mystery to her. He was only four years her junior, but he seemed to have vast amounts of knowledge about things that she didn't even think about. He was almost always engaged in some electronic activity, and all conversations revolved around the detailed folklore of a galaxy 'far, far away', or what to build in a strange, blockish virtual world. She had never really been sucked into the whole online role-play thing, but she supposed she had her own obsessions. Plus, when she was nine, her mother had not been away all the time, so they had done more things together as a family. Oscar's digital world held his focus now; it was his way of coping, and although she joined in occasionally, Ice mostly appreciated that it kept him busy and that she did not have to entertain him.

"If you mean the opening scene from 'Invasion of the Body Snatchers', I think you'll find that it should be, 'Hello, I'm from the 1950s'," she replied with emphasis, as Oscar tapped his phone back on. "Do you think Depton is full of alien plant replicants?" she continued. Still in movie mode, Oscar opened his mouth wide like a pod-person and pointed at her, making a hissing, rasping noise in response. Ice laughed at him and stared out of the window at the passers-by.

"What about him?" she said, indicating an elderly man trying not very successfully to keep dry with a battered, black umbrella and accompanied by a stocky, grizzled Staffordshire bull terrier. "Or them – I bet they are!" A couple of white-haired women were getting drenched, pushing their wheeled shopping trolleys towards the entrance of the supermarket car-park. The average age seemed to be about sixty. There had to be younger people here, though; Oscar's records had already been sent to the local primary school and she was going to join, annoyingly halfway through the second term, Year Nine at Depton High.

Depton itself was an uncomfortable mix of modern features, shoe-horned between the timeless brick buildings of a small Midlands town. Glass-fronted local shops offered electrical goods and furniture. These lined the main street, alongside pubs which advertised wide-screen viewing of the World Cup. On the right, they drove past the red awnings and neatly trimmed bay trees of an Indian restaurant, and just a bit further up, on the opposite side, the road was dominated by a massively overblown modern Catholic church next to a mid-Victorian house garishly converted into a take-away kebab shop. Ice noted with interest, two second-hand bookshops and a visitor's centre, and it reminded her that there were some features of Depton she was actually looking forward to.

"This town has a castle ruin, doesn't it, Dad?"

"Yes, indeed," he answered. "It's actually just over there – one of the oldest in the country I believe – though there's not an awful lot left of it. We can certainly put it on our list of things to see, once we're settled in."

"That'll be OK, then," thought Ice. She would check it out later – probably on her own. 'Ice by name, ice by nature,' was what Dad called her, referring to her seemingly cool reserve and lack of need for human company. It wasn't that she disliked people or didn't care about their feelings. On the contrary, Ice included all manner of living things in her circle – especially the creatures that most people considered worthy of extermination. Ice had let wasps drink lemonade from her fingertip before sending them on their way, rather than swatting at them or crushing them like most people did. Unlike flies (and humans), wasps always seemed to know which direction to go. Animals had clear, straightforward and honest thoughts and feelings and that made them much easier to deal with than people. She could almost always tell when people were lying – it was often and it was very tiring.

She leaned her head against the glass pane of the car. They were approaching the central feature – the clock-tower – which loomed over the town like an ancient monolith. Had there been any sunshine, it would have cast a gloomy shadow down the street. The time was accurate at least, she mused, checking the clock face. It was starting to get late and they'd

4

been sitting in the car for hours. Finishing this journey and getting to the house was becoming an increasingly welcome prospect, she thought, as she gazed up at the damp structure. She wasn't sure at what point she became aware of it, but as she continued to look, something small and unspeakably dark, unveiled itself from the shadowy side of the tawny sandstone and crept, spider-like, up the middle of the tower where it then sat, crouched like a tiny, black gargoyle, below the 'W' of the wind vane, clasping tightly to one of the stone decorations. Ice stared, feeling the cold surge of adrenalin cause a familiar sensation in the pit of her stomach, but she said nothing. Instead, silently, she observed the inky shape of the creature's head which turned as her father navigated the town's central island. Its eyes were not visible from the car, but Ice knew with a shudder that they were without a doubt fixed on her and her alone, and that they continued to watch her progress all the way up the rest of Depton High Street until the car turned off and they were out of view.

Chapter 2
The Dream

Getting to the new house after that, wasn't exactly an easy ride either. The detour signs were put up too late for the miserable drivers who encountered a white torrent of water at the town's flooded ford. They were forced to reverse, turn, and take an alternative route up and round the castle. Ice's father was quite grumpy by then and smacked his hands on the steering wheel, shouting that it was ridiculous and cursing the endless rain. By the time they had made several stops and starts and were winding their way through Depton's back streets, Ice was feeling car-sick and was tremendously grateful when they finally pulled up at the house and she could stumble out on to the tarred driveway, taking deep breaths to calm the reflex to retch. She was glad, too, that their new home was on a street that was high up and well away from the rising floodwater.

"Oh yeah! We're here!" Oscar called out, announcing the obvious.

"Thank goodness for that!" Ice replied. "I thought I was going to throw up!" The pounding of her pulse had calmed but her legs were wobbly. She was glad to be standing on solid ground at last.

They ran to the front porch as their father unlocked the door, and all stood dripping on the carpet of their new hallway. This was going to be home and Ice tried to persuade herself to be fine with that. How could it not be a wrench leaving the familiarity of her old house down south and the people she had known most of her life? But she pushed away those thoughts, before they became too strong, and focussed on the present. The house was nothing special – a 1930s semi-detached two-storey like thousands all over the country. Her mother had said they were good and solid and that's why they had lasted. As far as she was concerned, it was already fulfilling its prime function of keeping out the elements. Buddy seemed happy enough, too – he pushed past the three of them and shook himself dry in the hall before leading the way into the living room to find a suitable patch of carpet to lie on.

Much of their stuff was arriving the following day, so their first meal was a kind of indoor camping affair, sitting at the kitchen table on the stools that had been left by the previous owner, and eating beans on toast from brightly-coloured plastic plates. Their mother had always banned reading or texting at mealtimes and even though she wasn't there, the rule persisted. They were supposed to have time to communicate with each other – or at least that was the idea. Tonight, none of them was particularly chatty, each wrapped in their own thoughts.

Their father was probably worrying about the job – again. It was a source of constant stress and Ice wished that he would find something that didn't occupy his time and his mental space quite so much. It was bad enough when their mother was there, but then at least he seemed to enjoy being able to have a good moan with her about the company they both worked for. It was how they had met. She was in the legal department, he was a site engineer. Good jobs, good, steady incomes. Ice knew her life was easy and that they had everything they needed. She also knew that she needed to be grateful, but her mother was the main bread-winner, and these days her job took her away far more often than any of them liked. This time, she was in the USA, dealing with company contracts and sorting out their legal business. In her absence, Dad seemed to work more hours and see the two children less than ever. The shale gas company had asked them to relocate to Depton so that her father could be closer to the nearby drilling and fracturing site. It was a big deal having to move them all but it meant he would need to travel a lot less. At least the children would have one parent around some of the time. Mum would join them on her return.

Oscar, bereft of his phone, quickly shovelled in the morsels of food so that he could be excused and get back to texting or gaming or surfing or whatever it was that he did. Ice could not shake the unsettling feeling that had been generated by the strange events in town. She pushed away the disturbing image of the weird man, and most of all, tried to not think about the unreal creature watching her from the tower. She was quite keen to finish dinner, sort out what she needed for the new school the next day, have a bath and get to bed, such as it was. Whilst Oscar used technology, like most 21st Century children, Ice's refuge was books. She could immerse herself in them and become utterly absorbed, no matter what other unpleasant or annoying things were happening around her. It didn't matter if it was fiction or factual – reading had always been her best escape from boredom and a distraction from things she didn't want to think about. Tonight, though, she was intending to use her phone instead, to remind herself about the local area and look up its history. So far, she had mainly focussed on essential information like the route to school and where their house was. For the more interesting details, she had waited until they had definitely made the move. Now she was keen to find out a bit more.

Ice sent a text to her mother before settling in to do her research. She did not expect an immediate reply. That rarely

8

happened. Later, her mum would probably text her the view from the window – another hotel in another city. She looked at the local information site. Depton castle, it seemed, was pretty old, dating back to the 12th Century, and now mostly in ruins. Propped up on her temporary bed, Ice scrolled through the pictures of its angular, red sandstone towers, neatly manicured lawns and rough Tudor outhouses. Like so many buildings of heritage in England, it was thoroughly sanitised and well-kept for the tourists that arrived each summer from the USA and elsewhere to marvel at the 'oldness' of it all. For her part, Ice was more interested in the most ancient and least popular places of the world. She found it easy to visualise the former inhabitants – almost like they had left their imprint in the place – and was particularly fascinated to 'watch' the activities of the people of the ancient world before humans had begun to record their history, their lies, in writing.

Just as Ice was about to follow the link to further historical sites in the area, she stopped abruptly, feeling her pulse quicken. She brought the phone screen in closer and stared at one of the pictures on the screen. It was labelled, *'Peregrine on All Saints' Church'* and showed the bird of prey just taking off from a carving that jutted out at the top of the tower. It was not the shot of the bird that had startled her and grabbed her attention, though. It was the carving itself – a small, medieval gargoyle, weathered by age and acid rain and unmistakably like the creature Ice had tried to ignore earlier in the day. It couldn't be right. It had to be just one of those coincidences – a visual trick of the light. The creature she had 'seen' on Depton clock tower wasn't even real – it was just one of her weird imaginary things. They had been there as far back as she could remember and she had long since learned not to talk about them to the adults. Yet here, in front of her, was a carved depiction as if taken straight out of her own mind's eye. Ice spread her fingers across the screen to enlarge the image and stared at it for a good few minutes until she had convinced herself that it was, indeed, just a badly-worn artefact which could have been any of the hundreds of different gargoyle-type things sprouting from Gothic buildings all over Europe.

Ice's eyes at last began to close involuntarily, while she was surfing through pictures of local Neolithic stone circles, and she put down the phone. The bed was an inflatable camping mattress in the middle of the empty room, but really it was remarkably comfortable, and apart from the sound of gushing water, the street was quiet – which was a bonus. Though the window was without a curtain, yet and the still bucketing rain scattered the street-light into her room, it all failed to prevent Ice from falling into a dreamless sleep. Neither was she disturbed later, by her father's quiet footsteps past her door to his own room. At around one o'clock in the morning, the street-light went out and Ice began to dream. It was the same old dream of her childhood – first a low, rumbling, drumming sound, followed by the arrival of one, then more and then hundreds of small, dark shapes surrounding her. These were always accompanied by an overwhelming sense of dread. When she was very small, perhaps aged two or three, Ice had struggled to explain to her parents the reason why she so often appeared at the foot of their bed, crying. She had lacked the vocabulary to come up with much more than 'bad doggies' and so her confused parents had dismissed them as the normal night terrors most children experience at some point. Over time, Ice learned to cope with the dreams, and to keep quiet about the occasional daytime sighting, like today's.

Despite the fear that attended them, the creatures never threatened Ice nor harmed her in her dreams. Tonight, however, there was an oppressive clamouring and a suffocating, crowding feeling from which she struggled to wake. The rumbling, too, was becoming increasingly intense, and added to it now was another sound – a series of creaks and rattles. Ice kicked her feet against the edges of the sleeping bag and clawed her way to consciousness, gasping as she woke up. For a moment, she believed that Oscar was playing a trick on her, shaking the mattress, but the movement was not quite right. She had the sensation that she was being slid back and forth across the floor and the rumbling sound had not stopped. Ice sat up, put her hands down on either side of the mattress and found that the whole room was moving.

It was with a mixture of alarm and fascination that Ice realised they were experiencing an earth tremor. She had learned about earthquakes in Geography lessons and on the school trip to the Science Museum, they had found it hilarious standing in the earthquake simulator as it shook them from side to side. This was like that, but without the laughter of her friends. Now she could hear Buddy barking excitedly and Oscar shouting, "What the hell was that?" The tremors died down and Ice moved to get up off the bed. The street light was still off, but the rain clouds had parted for a moment and a bright half-moon had risen. Silhouetted in the window, was one of the dream creatures; it sat watching Ice, with a pair of coldly luminous eyes. As she caught sight of it, she could have sworn it raised one of its long, taloned 'fingers', pointed it at her and then waggled it slowly back and forth as though giving her a tiny warning.

"Did you feel that?" Oscar said, bursting into her room and causing Ice to turn suddenly. When she looked back to the window, the creature was gone.

Chapter 3
Battery Operated Boy

When they had waited long enough until they felt there were going to be no more tremors, and Buddy had stopped his low growling, they tried to recapture the sleep that had been so dramatically disturbed. By breakfast time, however, it was obvious that the three of them were feeling the effects of the combined events of the previous day and night. All were awake and seeking cereal or cups of tea far earlier than they needed, but it was good that it wasn't going to be a rush to get to their new schools on their first day. Oscar had the bright-eyed, flushed look of too much excitement and too little sleep and was pretty much carrying on a conversation single-handedly.

"That earthquake was awesome! I didn't know they could have quakes in England like that. D'you think we're on a fault line or something? What if there's a mega volcano buried deep below us? How much do you think that was on the Richter scale? I reckon it was about a five or a nine or something. You could hear the windows rattling – I wonder if it made any cracks." Even though they had checked the night before, he looked round the kitchen as if he hoped to find signs of destruction. There wasn't much. There was nothing that could have fallen from the empty cupboards, and the single kettle, plus their three mugs, had managed to stay in their places on the laminated surface of the built-in kitchen table. The only sign that there had been any disturbance was a small pile of plaster that had fallen from the ceiling into the sink. Ice's father hoped it didn't indicate anything more serious structurally.

"It wasn't really an earthquake, Oscar. Lucky for us!" Ice replied, "and we do have tremors in England now and then, you know." She said this with seeming authority, even though she had never experienced one before. It was quite fun to be reminded of the power of the natural world when it was just a little 'tasterquake' like this one, but it was also comforting to know that England had never been at the centre of anything really big.

Ice's father nodded in agreement, sipping his tea and checking his phone for the time.

"Ice, will you be OK going into school today? Do you want me to come with you or do you not want me being all parenty and embarrassing on your first day? I can drop you off, of course." He dug around in his case for some paperwork. "The letter here says just turn up at the reception and someone will show you the way to where you're supposed to register, etc."

Ice thought about this for a moment, weighing up the moral support of having her father with her, against the impression this would give the other children already at the school. She knew he wasn't as relaxed as his attitude seemed to suggest. Dad hadn't become so distant that he wouldn't know what a challenge it would be to go to a new school in a new town but he was trying to make it feel like it wasn't a scary thing. He was probably right, though. It was better not to be seen with her 'Daddy' taking her in. She decided that if he gave her a lift, she would take it from there.

"That's fine, Dad," Ice said, though she felt less fine than she seemed. "You need to go in with Oscar anyway, don't you? You don't mind him being 'parenty and embarrassing' do you, Oscar?"

"Ooh, hilarious!" Oscar said, without expression, picking up his phone. He was glad that the primary school were expecting his Dad to come in on his first day.

"Of course," their father replied and he gave Ice a small nod – perhaps thanks or an attempt at reassurance.

Buddy needed walking before they left. He was already pushing his muzzle against Ice's knee in frustration. She bent down to give him a hug, even while she knew that she shouldn't. Hugs were a monkey thing. To dogs, they were uncomfortable and rude and it was lucky that Buddy was so tolerant. He wriggled while Ice buried her nose in the warm fur of his neck. He always smelled sweet like biscuits, she thought – not the strong doggy odour of some of the pets she had met.

"I'll take Buddy out, now," she offered. "Will he be OK at home today, alone in a new house?"

Her father considered this for a moment. He seemed to be weighing something up, but she wasn't sure if was whether she should take Buddy out alone or the answer to her question. She used to walk him in their old neighbourhood – from the age of 11. She wasn't going to get lost!

"Thanks, Ice," he answered. "Half hour max. Don't worry about him – I'm going to be home some of the day – I have to be here for the removals delivery of our stuff."

After that, her dad was true to his word and said 'goodbye' to her outside the gate. Next to it, was the green and white school sign – the unoriginal title of 'Depton High School' and the local authority badge, indicating she was in the right place. From all directions, her new fellow pupils were arriving in noisy friendship clusters or as individuals engrossed in their phones. Some of them observed her with mild interest as they passed, maybe noticing her new uniform and her hesitant expression. Ice felt the same queasy discomfort she always did in social situations and it was made worse by the large number of people all heading towards the main buildings. She mentally instructed herself to ignore the knotted feeling in the pit of her stomach and the nagging urge to walk up the road away from the school gate; it was important to be as normal as possible.

"Be Ice," she thought, forcing herself to breathe calmly, despite her elevated heart-rate. She gripped the straps of her backpack and moved off rather quickly up the curved path towards the school reception.

As so often was the case, her anxiety was unnecessary. Of course they were expecting her, and a semblance of school efficiency took over as Ice was guided by one of the office staff to her form room, where a male teacher was taking the register. Ice judged that he must have been one of the older members of staff, perhaps close to retirement. He was obviously one of those men who was never going to go bald, but instead had thick, completely white hair worn in a brushed-back style. His jacket, which was hanging over the back of the teacher's chair, had old-fashioned leather patches on the elbows. Like some host on a game show about antiques, he was not only wearing a burgundy waistcoat but a bow tie as well. He seemed to be expecting her and gave a nod and a lift of the eyebrows to acknowledge her arrival.

"Ah hello! Is it Isis?" he asked, gesturing her in and making Ice wince at her given name. "Welcome. I'm Mr Ward, your form tutor. Find yourself a seat anywhere and I'll sort you out with your timetable and some escorts for the day. Just let me finish the register."

Ice scanned the room. She knew that it was full of individuals watching her with interest, but for her it was like looking across a landscape of randomly-shaped, anonymous features. Finding a seat was easier said than done; it was the kind of decision Ice hated being asked to make. Would it be considered weirdly over-familiar if she sat next to a pupil where there was a space, or would it be worse if she behaved unsociably and sat at a separate desk? Just as it was beginning to be even more awkward by her inaction, she was rescued by a voice.

"Hi! There's a space here – though we won't be in this room for long. First period starts in five minutes."

Ice moved over quickly and sat down, giving the speaker a grateful smile, and a whispered, "Hi."

Her rescuer's impact on Ice was immediate. The girl was slight and brown. Her straight hair was fringed and cropped just above her shoulders. It was very dark – almost black – as were the irises of her eyes, reminding Ice of a manga heroine. She was most struck, though, by the authenticity of the girl's smile as she nodded Ice into the spare seat.

"I'm Mia. Are you really called Isis?"

"It's a long story," whispered Ice, "just call me Ice."

"Cool!" Mia replied, "Like a comic supervillain," and she giggled.

"Er, not so much!" Ice smiled wryly in return.

"Well you can tell me about it at lunch-time. You can eat with us, if you like. Are you sandwiches or are you eating in the canteen? Most of us go in there or sit out under the cover." Mia had a strong Birmingham accent. Ice liked it.

"Actually, I didn't have a chance to make lunch. It would be great if you could show me the canteen at lunchtime and stop me from being Norma No-Mates on my first day!" Ice was only half joking. The only thing worse than putting up with a lot of people, was being among them but awkwardly and noticeably on your own.

Mr Ward was handing her something on a piece of paper.

"Here you are, Isis – this is your timetable for the week. Mia, since you're already getting acquainted, would you mind showing Isis to her first class? Isis it's all there – rooms and times. If you get lost, just ask anyone, but it's fairly straightforward. I'm afraid you'll have to be thrown in pretty much at the deep end, arriving in the middle of the term like this. You can see form period is at the start of every day, so if you need anything you can ask." Mr Ward's accent reflected his clothing; it wouldn't have been out of place as the voice-over for an old black and white information film.

Ice nodded as she took the paper and thanked him. She felt a wave of nostalgia for the familiarity of the form room in her previous school, her classmates and the old routines. Starting again was hard.

The best thing about the rest of the morning was that it was dedicated to academic stuff. If she could put her efforts into thinking about the content of the lessons, it made it easier not to dwell on the complex and challenging events that had led her to this point. Some of the classes, like English, were covering different books or topics to her old school and though she loved reading, she felt a little lost and would need time to catch up. Others, like maths or science, were much the same. Ice was lucky. She didn't want to be thought of as a 'geek' but she had the knack of remembering what she had read or seen and she really did like learning new things. The 'Old Dragon' of an English teacher in her previous school had taught the pupils, 'Knowledge is Strength', and Ice thought she understood what it meant. The more things you knew, the more you could make choices.

You could put things together. See the bigger picture. Make links.

The social side that morning turned out to be less of a strain than she had predicted. Although there were curious glances from the other pupils in her classes and the occasional question about where she had come from and why, they had been friendly enough. Ice judged that she had done a fine job of answering and sounding as normal and relaxed as possible. The first few lessons went by quickly. She was feeling a great deal more settled and hungry by the time she sought out Mia in the canteen.

For a moment she stood in the doorway looking in at the mass of people, unable to spot her new acquaintance but it couldn't have been more than a few seconds before she was grabbed by the arm and swept in by Mia who took two metal trays and gave one to Ice.

"Was your morning OK?" She asked. "I'll introduce you to some people in a minute. Don't worry – I was new last year. It didn't take me long to settle in and now I feel like I've been here ages."

Ice gave a half smile, nodding her agreement. Mia was telling the truth, but she was clearly very socially adept; she had an easy, friendly manner, unlike Ice for whom every interaction required conscious effort. The noise levels were building in the canteen as they took their trays to their seat and sat down at a table with a couple of pupils who were introduced briefly to Ice.

"Daniel and Emma from my English class," Mia said. "This is Ice. She's new today."

They both gave a little wave of greeting.

"Ice... as in the cold stuff?" Daniel queried. "Is that your actual name or a nickname?"

Ice sighed inwardly. She wondered how many times she'd have to repeat this conversation over the next few weeks. "My mum is a fan of Ancient Egypt. My real name is Isis after the goddess, you know? They've always called me Ice though. My dad says it suits my character. I don't know if that's true, but these days, when people hear the word 'ISIS' they don't immediately think of the ancient goddess – they think of that terrorist group from before, so it's best to stick to the shortened version!"

"Yeah – no problem!" Daniel replied, waving his plastic fork at her. "Well I'm Daniel or Dan. Just don't call me Danny!"

"OK, Danny!" Teased Mia, ruffling his scruffy, dirty-blonde hair. Ice took a bite out of her pizza.

She was interrupted by a sudden commotion at the other side of the room. At first it was difficult to make out the cause, but then she saw that a group had gathered around a boy. He could have been a Year 7 pupil but looked very small for his age.

"Oh no!" Mia groaned, pulling a face of distaste. "They're teasing Bob, again – poor little guy."

"What?" Ice was beginning to see that something was not right.

"Battery Operated Boy," Daniel answered, "He is a bit odd. He makes funny noises sometimes, you know, like a little robot – battery operated? That's why the older kids bully him a bit. It's not fair really."

"He's got special needs," interjected Mia. "They know they're not meant to do that to him!"

Ice was on her feet, metal tray in hand. She could feel anger rising like a hissing, dizzying flood. Before she could sufficiently realise what she was doing, her fury at the bullies had brought her face to face with them. Battery Operated Boy had his hands up to his ears and was, indeed, making a low-pitched humming noise. Some boys were gathered round him. One was poking at his chest with a fork.

"Come on, Bob. Don't you have any other settings? What about if I push this button?" Other children were standing by with looks of disapproval, but nobody was doing anything to stop them. Ice gripped her tray by its upturned edge and raised it in one swift movement, striking the closest boy across his laughing face and knocking him sideways into one of his companions. A girl nearby screamed and the room fell into a hush; all turned towards Ice, their faces a mixture of shock and morbid delight.

Chapter 4
Exclusion

"Ice – what the hell did you think you were doing?" Her father had been silently driving for a good few minutes, seething, before being able to bring himself to remonstrate with her. "Have you any idea what sort of trouble you could be in? That boy's parents could press charges for assault!"

Ice did know. She had sat in the head's office, listening to all the ways in which she was in trouble while she waited for her father to come and pick her up. Various witnesses had been questioned as were all the boys involved. Some of them had tried to deny that there had been anything going on, but Ice had made it easy for the head by not hiding the truth at all. The older boy, Joe, had been more shocked than seriously hurt although Ice's tray had left a red mark on his cheek which would probably be an incriminating bruise by the morning. She had not even tried to explain herself. Instead, hiding her mortified expression behind the curtain of her long hair, she had nodded along to the reprimands and the decision to give her a day's exclusion for her actions. Apparently the school had a 'strong policy on bullying' and pupils were to report incidents to an adult, not take matters into their own hands. Whatever the policy was, Ice thought, it wasn't protecting people. Mia and Daniel had also been questioned. Ice had not heard what they said and they could not meet her eye when they left the head's office. Had she lost some friendships before they had even started? It was Joe's reluctance to talk about it, and the fact that 'BOB' was the son of the chair of governors and a local councillor, that had saved her from a more serious punishment. As it was, she wondered what would happen when Joe's parents found out.

"I know, Dad. I'm sorry – it was really stupid."

"Ice, I recognise that you have a strong sense of justice and all that, but you've got to be more sensible about your reactions. I know it's not been easy with your mother… you know… and you're just into that really difficult teenage thing… I get that. Just… well… bloody hell, Ice! You can't start knocking people about with kitchenware!''

Ice was not going to cry. The reference to her mother was a low blow and a surprise – a testament to just how upset her father was. But acts of cruelty always made her furious; though she felt ashamed at herself, she was also still seething – why did people get away with victimising the small and vulnerable? When she was younger, there had been moments her parents had described as 'melt-down'. It was always when there was something happening that Ice had felt was wrong, but had no power to stop. Over the years she had learned the 'Be Ice' technique and had never actually hit anyone before, but there was something about BOB that resonated with her. She knew what it was like to be alone in a crowd – to be the only one who was different in a room full of people. Many of her classmates at her old school had known her since they were at nursery together. They hadn't cared that she was a bit 'odd'. Perhaps they had never noticed. But in new social situations, she tended to be a little bit aloof. Had she over-reacted because of her own feelings of being displaced and awkward? Her actions, she conceded, hadn't helped and had let the bully off by turning him into the victim. The trouble was, she couldn't think rationally in those moments. Ice sighed. Being 'ice' only worked up to a point and now damage had been done. She was shocked at how quickly her actions had changed things and she vowed she would not use physical violence again.

***

"Oh, what now?" Her father's exclamation interrupted her thoughts. "This is all I need!"

Ice glanced up at him and then out of the car window. A motley group of people was gathered in front of the town hall, obstructing the traffic. Her father pressed on the horn in annoyance but took his foot off the accelerator pedal, careful not to make contact with the stragglers that were across the road.

"Damned tree-hugging hippies!" Ice's dad mouthed his frustration at the milling crowd. They were carrying hand-painted and printed signs bearing slogans like, 'No Drill, No Spill', 'Stop Poisoning my Children' and 'Keep the Frack out of our Water'.

Some of the participants did have a 'hippy' look about them: there was a bearded man wearing a multi-coloured waistcoat and striped, baggy trousers. He had a faded, red bandana tied round his head. One woman had on an orange beret, sandals and a long, floral skirt. But others seemed more 'normal'; they could easily have been those little old ladies who had just finished their shopping, or people at a music festival wearing jeans and T-shirts. A few were obviously mothers with young children.

"Is that your company they're protesting about, Dad?" Ice inquired. Her father nodded grumpily. He was in no mood to get into that conversation. He was simply one of the engineers whose job it was to oversee the hydraulic equipment which injected the gel; he had to make sure it ran smoothly and efficiently and that the ground crew knew everything they needed to know. It had been tough when the ban had been in place but the industry had restarted with a set of new regulations that were designed to make it much safer than before. He had been one of the lucky ones with the right skills at the right time to walk back into a good job. He wasn't a denier. Ice's father knew that things were not ideal – people had definitely had an impact on the environment – but he had a job to do. As far as he was concerned, he wasn't interested in politics and just at this moment he had no time for eco-warriors shoving their views down his throat. Right now they had enough worries. The floods were going to force them to stop drilling and temporarily close the site.

"When we get home, I need you to go to your room, Ice," he instructed, as they finally turned into their road. "I was right in the middle of receiving the delivery of all our stuff when the school phoned. I could really have done without this today!"

"OK," Ice acquiesced. If anything, his mood seemed to be blackening, along with the sky which was now a murky, ominous slate colour – a prelude to yet another downpour.

As it happened, the plan to go straight to her room was scrapped. Buddy was bouncing up and down, frantic for a walk and desperate to investigate all the boxes and larger furniture which had been offloaded by the removal company and which now littered the driveway. Dad had come back from work to meet the lorry and they had been halfway through unloading when he had been called in to school. By the time he and Ice arrived home, the delivery men had finished clearing the lorry and were waiting to carry items inside so that they could sign off the job. Ice found her bicycle. Using the map on her phone, she located the town park which turned out to be a popular place for dog-walkers and rode there with Buddy pulling her on the lead. Her dad would have disapproved of this risky behaviour but he was distracted by the loading in. Buddy was delighted to play boisterous dog games with the neighbourhood pets and they were lucky today. None of the owners were the frightened type who clipped their own dog on the lead as soon as they saw him.

On return, she fed and watered Buddy before helping with the unpacking. The removal men had helped to bring in all the large items of furniture and now Ice worked in unison with her father to square things away in the downstairs rooms and stack boxes up until they made cardboard towers against each wall. By the time they had finished, the rain was descending in torrents again and it was time to fetch Oscar. Ice was left to sort out the kitchen equipment and to 'think seriously' about her actions.

She ripped open boxes marked 'cutlery' and sorted knives and forks into trays. She put away the two bags of groceries which had been left on the kitchen cabinet and then found and hauled upstairs, the box containing the old desktop computer, keyboard and screen. This belonged to her mother and Ice liked it. Though it was big and cumbersome and beginning to be a bit temperamental, it was quicker and easier to type on a proper keyboard and see things on a big screen. Mobile phones had their uses but they were pretty fiddly. It didn't take long to set it up on the table next to her bed and cable it together. Dad had insisted that the Internet company set up for immediate access, so it was easy enough to get it connected to the hub. She had opened several unrelated websites on 'shale gas fracturing' and 'Warwickshire history', when she heard her father's key in the front door. The rain, which for days had fallen in a continuous drenching stream, seemed to be making up for its morning break and was now reaching a deafening crescendo on the rooftops and on the drowned pavement outside. Ice scrolled through the information pages. There were sites of special scientific interest, wildlife groups, places to walk, etc., but she was intrigued by a link to *'Myths and Legends of Old Warwickshire'*. She had just clicked on it when she was surprised to hear a female voice downstairs.

Ice let go of the mouse and left her room to peer down at the visitor. Her father was ushering in a woman and a small boy who was wiping his shoes repeatedly and methodically on the doormat. With a surge of interest, Ice realised that it was BOB. She watched as her father said something to Oscar who then bounded up the stairs, shouting, "Ice, Dad wants you! There's somebody here!"

She was already part of the way down the stairs when Oscar met her and turned, half leading and half getting in the way, back down.

"Who's that? What did you do? Are you in trouble?"

"No. It's just a boy from my school," she replied, tetchily. "I didn't do anything to him!"

Ice followed Oscar into the kitchen where their father had taken BOB and the woman. The adults were sitting at the kitchen table and both looked up as she entered.

"Ice, this is Mrs Bennett – Nathan's mother."

For a moment Ice was confused before realising that her father was referring to Battery Operated Boy. Nathan was his proper name, of course!

"Oh hello, Ice! I wanted to thank you for today," the woman said, smiling. She had the same tightly curled, dark hair as Nathan, and as she spoke, she attempted to make it a

27

little less wet, rubbing it with her hands and flicking small droplets of rainwater into the air. "I've been trying to get them to listen to me about the bullying for ages. They keep telling me that they are doing all they can but then it still goes on." She turned to Ice's father and continued, "And thank you for giving permission for the school to let me have your contact details. I didn't mean to intrude, but I felt I ought to say something."

"Ice is in quite a lot of trouble," her father interjected. "We don't actually condone violence."

"No, of course not. I'm not saying that – but you stood up for him, Ice, and I'm grateful. It needed something. Nathan doesn't always understand what they're doing or why – he hasn't got the same level of social awareness as most kids his age. Maybe the bullies will think twice now."

Nathan was staring at Ice in a candid, unselfconscious way – the way of very young children. She sensed intelligence behind the look, but so far he had observed it all in silence and she was a little taken aback when he spoke. He had an unexpectedly low, clear voice and talked in a precise way as though he was explaining something complicated to someone who might not understand. She was reminded of her friend Thomas from her old school. He had stood up in class one day and told them all that he had an announcement to make. All the children and the teacher had turned to look at him and he had proceeded to let them know that he was autistic.

"I've been diagnosed," he had said, bluntly. That's why I like some things so much and why I get stressed about some stuff."

The class hadn't reacted. Most of them had known Thomas since they were four years old. When he had finished, the teacher had said, "OK, Tom. Thanks for that.

Now back to the history of the Aztecs." Ice liked Thomas – he was the most honest person she knew. It was an unpleasant pang to think of those she had left behind. Nathan's dry manner was a little like the way her old friend used to speak.

"Well, basically," he said, "there are these boys that sometimes push on my jumper, like this..." he turned his index finger on himself, demonstrating. "Sometimes they laugh too loudly near me and make my ears hurt and they get in front of me and stop me walking."

"I saw that. Are you OK, though?" Ice asked.

"Well, basically, I am OK. That boy should not push on my jumper. I don't think it is appropriate that he does that. When they laugh too loud, I don't think they should be so loud. I saw you – you are a new girl in our school. Basically, you put your tray on his face, like this…". Nathan gave a perfect impression of Ice's misdemeanour,"…and then he stopped pushing on my jumper and that boy stopped laughing."

Oscar gave out a little snort of amusement but Nathan seemed not to notice. Ice's father listened, switching his attention between the speakers and seeming to relax his attitude a little, after hearing the other side of the story and accepting Mrs Bennett's thanks.

"Well I really appreciate you coming to tell Ice. Thanks for that. Ice has always stood up for people – I'm just disappointed that she's made a bad impression on her first day. Um… as you can see, it's a bit chaotic here still, but I can offer you a cup of tea before you brave the elements again."

Buddy had done his normal trick of pinning guests to their chairs and was lying under the table on Mrs Bennett's feet. Nathan obviously decided that his mother was accepting the offer to have a cup of tea. He nodded, walked out of the kitchen and headed up the stairs. Ice's dad stretched out his arm and intercepted Oscar just as he was about to follow, but he let Ice go up. Nathan seemed curious about the disordered house. Downstairs was still a jumble of large items that they hadn't taken upstairs yet.

"Er… that's my bedroom. I know it's a bit empty still. Our stuff only arrived today, but we haven't got all the upstairs furniture yet," Ice said as Nathan wandered into her room. She would normally have felt extremely uncomfortable with anyone invading her territory like this, but the combination of the room's emptiness and Nathan's odd lack of awareness made her less bothered about her privacy.

He stood just inside the door, on the bare floorboards, and scanned the room, turning his head in a slow, deliberate movement from right to left.

"Your room still needs some things. Well… basically, you're going to put some furniture in it when you've moved it upstairs. You have the bed there and you need a wardrobe and a carpet." He spoke in a matter-of-fact voice and indicated the places where he felt the furniture should be placed. "You've got a picture of a creaker." Nathan had not changed his tone but was pointing in the direction of the computer. Ice glanced over at the screen. It was open on the *'Myths and Legends'* webpage and showed a book-cover depicting a mythical creature. It was alarmingly familiar. The artist had given it two upward-sloping eyes, glowing bright against a dark, featureless face, and had painted it perched on its haunches, resting its 'hands' on its knees and gripping a mossy rock with long, thin toes.

"What… creak… what?" Ice looked intently at the screen and then back at Nathan.

"There are lots of creakers," Nathan replied, indifferent to her surprise and continuing in his business-like way. "Well… basically, there were some before and then there are lots more that I've seen now."

"You've seen them?" Ice was still not sure if Nathan was talking about the computer or his imagination or… something else. She read the title of the book on the screen: 'The Depton Shadelings and other Myths of the Midlands'.

"Seen them!" He nodded, imitating Ice's emphasis. "All around." He wiggled his fingers and waved his arms in front of him and above his head, as if showing Ice invisible creatures about the room. "Outside."

Ice knew he was not lying.

Chapter 5
The Book

That night all three exhausted themselves getting more furniture up the stairs and arranging the bedrooms. At least tonight they had a proper bed to sleep on. Her father had calmed down considerably and had given Ice his disappointed but understanding talk. She was to stay off school the following day and would then need to report to her form tutor for a week, to ensure she was settling in properly and was 'behaving appropriately'. Oscar pressed her for the gory details, demonstrating the impressed admiration of a nine-year-old for anyone taking on the 'big guys', though he was a bit jealous. He couldn't see why a day off school was a punishment, and every now and then, when he caught Ice's eye, he pretended to hit someone with an invisible tray, accompanying it with a 'whack!' sound.

Ice woke the following day, unreasonably positive. There had been no visitations in her dreams in the night. In fact she couldn't remember having any dreams at all. She looked outside. The damp pavements were now steaming in the sunshine.

"Huh! Lucky! You get a day off school!" Oscar reminded her unnecessarily, whilst pouring himself milk on his cereal. "Maybe I should hit someone with a tray…"

"Maybe you should hurry up if you want a lift to school!" their father responded. "Ice, please walk the dog and then you're to stay here – I have to lock down the site today and then go in to head office. There's nothing else I can do. You'll be fine. I'll check in with you when I can. Keep your phone on and handy. Don't answer the door to anyone."

Ice replied that she would and that she would be OK. Though it would be a bit odd in the empty house, her own company for a day was not a problem and she had plans – if she had to miss school, she was going to make the most of the time.

When they had left, Ice gave Buddy his walk. Even though she would have done this before school anyway, she felt conspicuous, like everyone was looking at her. She was glad when they had closed the front door again and she and Buddy had gone back upstairs. The computer was now on a desk by the window and she turned it on and sat down. She was interested to pick up the two threads of research that had been interrupted the previous day. The first was related to her father's job: she knew her father was an engineer for a company that did drilling for 'shale gas' and she remembered when it had been suspended and her father had been out of work briefly, though her mother had continued to work in the company's legal department. When they had started up again, Ice had assumed, stupidly perhaps, that the problems had been sorted out. But those people on the street the previous day had disturbed her. They had seemed very angry with the company still and Ice felt she needed to know why.

She typed 'drilling shale gas' into the search engine, skipped the academic sounding articles and clicked on the link that seemed to explain what it was. She read:

Shale gas is an increasingly important source of energy in the USA and worldwide. Although gas has long been extracted from natural cracks in the rock, modern technology in hydraulic fracturing (or fracking) has resulted in a boom in recent years.

Ice recognised some of the terminology. She had heard her father talking about 'hydraulics' before and she had seen 'fracking' on the news. She knew it was connected with her parents' work but her father had always dismissed the scare stories. She wasn't completely clear why people were protesting. Ice went back to the search engine and tried 'protests fracking'. This brought up several links to organisations opposed to the industry, along with newspaper articles about protestors blockading council offices and obstructing traffic. With a sudden rush of accomplishment, Ice noticed a headline from the 'Depton Herald'.

Locals protest Warwickshire fracking site.

Local protesters have been gathering outside the council offices for a month to protest the controversial drilling process.

"This is putting our children's health at risk," one of the protestors said.

Depton town councillor, Anna King said: "The county council has totally let us down on this. They seem to be completely indifferent to the threat to our community."

"What threat?" Ice wondered. She was annoyed with her own ignorance. But that was often the way. Things that were close to home were often the ones we scrutinised the least. Ice typed in another search which brought up links to American sites showing videos of people setting fire to water as it came out of the tap. Others complained that they had become sick since the drilling had started. Ice read, unable to suppress a surge of alarm, that some places had reported a link between fracking and earthquakes. She didn't know how many of these stories were true. Even though she could tell that the people in the videos weren't lying, they might have simply believed what they were experiencing was linked to the drilling. Ice knew how easily people fell for 'fake news' and saw connections that weren't really there. They were always looking for somebody or something to blame. She would ask her dad more when he got back.

She felt a little underhand checking up on her parents' work in this way, but they had never particularly discussed it with her and Oscar, and now she felt like they had not been totally honest. Her next task, however, required her to be outright disobedient. She had promised to stay in the house, but now she took the keys from the hook in the hallway and let herself out of the front door. It was already lunch time and she hoped that nobody would spot her walking from her house to the bookshops in the High Street. She had felt awkward outside earlier, before school, but she would be much more obvious now – a thirteen-year-old in town at this time of day during the term. In her head she ran through all manner of reasons why she might be allowed out at lunch. If they asked, she would say that her dad was just in the car. In typical English fashion, however, nobody even batted an eyelid when she pushed open the door of the first bookshop, causing the suspended bell to ring. Ice looked up and down the aisles. She instantly liked the shop. It had that very distinctive smell and was full of old and local-interest books. It would have been easy to lose herself for a couple of hours among the crammed shelves. There was a second-hand hardback all about the castle, and a slim volume of popular walks around the area. Today, she was searching for only one – the one she had seen online.

"Are you looking for something in particular?" A short, grey-haired, middle-aged woman was standing behind the till and finally addressed Ice after she had been studying the shelves for a couple of minutes.

Ice crossed over to the counter.

"I'm looking for a book called, *'The Depton Shadelings…'*"

"*… and other Myths of the Midlands,'*" the woman finished. "Yes, we have it – or we did. Let me just check..."

She disappeared into a back room and came out a while later with a box. In it were about twenty dusty copies of the book Ice was looking for.

"Perhaps I should put some back on the shelf," the woman mused as she handed Ice a copy. "£7.99."

Ice was examining the painting on the cover. More detail was visible than she had been able to see the previous night on the computer image. It was well-painted, she thought, though now that she could see it more clearly, not exactly like her own dream animals. The artist had, however, captured the creature's shadowy quality because apart from the main, central depiction, several others were just visible, half merged with the dark background.

She paid, thanked the shop assistant and left quickly, already reading, which she proceeded to do all the way home as she walked, glancing up only now and then to watch where she was going and avoid walking into things.

Chapter 6
Mysteries

Ice reached the driveway to the new house. Her heart was pounding by this time, but not from the exercise. The book was a mix of ghost tales and mysteries of the local area; she could see they were intended as entertaining bits of mythology along the lines of the Loch Ness Monster or Big Foot. There was a story about the ghost of a woman who had thrown herself from the tower at the castle, and another about a giant, savage cow with eyes of flame, that was slain by Guy of Warwick. Ice skimmed these rapidly, leafing through until she found the title story. It was written in the same mock sensational tone designed to both amuse and horrify the reader, but as Ice absorbed the other-worldly details, she steadied herself against the brick gate-post, and took deep breaths to stop the trembling in her hands. Her 'imaginary' dream creatures were there before her on the pages of the book, in accounts of sightings going back thousands of years:

The tales told of ghostly 'creaking' and 'hissing' sounds heard all around Depton and the surrounding countryside. The origin of this eerie noise was, according to local people, the 'Depton Shadelings', which supposedly had their lair under nearby Mort's Hill. The name 'shadeling' covered a host of stories of ethereal 'cat-like' creatures or 'phantom dogs' which haunted the area. In one case from the 1800s, a young maid, hurrying home one evening, was supposed to have seen several of these animals in one night, only to witness them vanish into the hill. She had counted herself lucky not to have been lured by them into the underworld. Apparently there had been random disappearances of people from time to time. When people went missing, locals would say they'd been taken by the shadelings who they said were demons and that there was an entrance to Hell located on the hill.

Folklore associated with dark forces in the area seemed to stretch back in time. Mort's hill itself was the site of an old Iron Age camp, but the creatures had been spotted also at the Twelve Brothers – the prehistoric stone circle nearby – and were perhaps even linked to its construction, many thousands of years ago. The ancient peoples, the text said, may have built it as a place of worship or 'appeasement through sacrificial acts', meaning they might have killed and buried things, thinking it would win the approval of the creatures. Bones of various animals had been unearthed around the area.

Some of the tales of the creatures were of miraculous escapes from death, or help for lost travellers, but many were more sinister, associating them with the Devil and foretelling disaster and destruction. One photograph showed a stained-glass window from the old church. Two pious individuals, a man and a woman, dressed in medieval clothes, had their hands clasped in prayer and their eyes focused on the symbol of the cross, while at their feet lurked five 'satanic' forms – the shadelings. The saddest story was that of a local woman in her 70s who was murdered as a witch in 1952. She had lived a reclusive life and had apparently been 'conversing' with the wildlife. The murderer had stabbed her through the neck with a pitchfork. Whoever had done it had never been discovered.

It was difficult for Ice to know what to feel. The 'shadelings' had to be real – they were not figments of her imagination! They had been seen by people like her throughout the centuries, though she did not know why they were invisible to most. It was a kind of thrill to discover their reality, but it was alarming, too. Were they portents of doom, as some of the legends told? Did it mean terrible things were going to happen because she had seen one on arrival in Depton? Ice was not superstitious as a rule but she could not stop the feeling of unease and isolation that welled up. How could she tell anyone without being considered mad or a witch like the poor old lady in the book – or more likely, thought to be simply making it up?

The book contained several hand-drawn maps of the area. Ice scrutinised these, and one in particular – the one showing the stone circle, less than two miles from her house, accessible on the canal towpath. She could visit it now and still be back before her family. Suppressing her feelings of guilt at her disobedience, Ice memorised the route, clipped the book to the carrier on her bike and pedalled towards the canal.

It was an exhilarating experience, cycling along the towpath. In places it had been worn down into gullies by a century of horses' hooves and the countless feet of pedestrians. Ice had to concentrate hard to navigate carefully and avoid hitting her head on the low bridges that crossed the canal every few hundred metres. The opaque, brown water was kept at a constant level by a series of locks and gates, but the river could occasionally be seen alongside or below the canal and was hurtling fiercely over the weir and spreading out across the low-lying meadows. By the time Ice reached the gate that led into the field, her hands were aching – she hadn't realised how tightly she'd been gripping the handlebars.

The stone circle was both remarkable and underwhelming. Here it still stood, dug and cut and carried and heaved upright by humans of a bygone millennium and yet a simple, unannounced set of pitted, grey-white rocks in the middle of someone's field of stubbly wheat. It took Ice's breath away, nevertheless. She had that knack, after all, of envisaging the long-gone business of humans and other creatures in places like these. Now she half closed her eyes and squinted at the site. The stones became smoother and more regular, their surfaces covered with earthy decorations and green garlands. Within the circle, she could picture a group of people gathered, facing the direction of the setting sun. As each stone cast its elongated shadow, she imagined small, dark forms which seemed to emerge from the earth and disappear as though leaping and diving through the waves of the sea. Ice wondered about the ancient people of the time. She was sure they had been able to see and respond to the presence of the creatures. In her visualisation, in front of each stone was a freshly-dug pit into which something was carefully laid as each was touched by the dying light of the sun.

As if to illustrate the sudden fragility of the normal world, the ground beneath Ice's feet literally began to move, knocking her to her knees. She let go of the bicycle and clutched at the pebbly earth in front of her. The tremor passed as suddenly as it started – lasting only a few seconds – but Ice waited, afraid to stand until everything felt solid again. The truth was, she knew that was never going to happen. The creatures of her imagination were real. The normal rules had been broken, even if the earthquakes themselves never returned.

Her phone buzzed in her back pocket. It was her father.

"Ice are you OK? Is everything alright in the house?" Ice lied that everything was fine, not giving away her location, nor that she felt shaken by more than the physical tremors of the earth.

"Just stay inside. It's nothing to worry about. Look after Buddy," he added, briefly. "I'll see you later."

Ice was long past the age where she trusted the judgement of adults about what to worry about, but she had no choice. She stood, brushed herself down, picked up the book and the bicycle from where she had dropped them and let herself back through the gate on to the towpath.

She was perched on a stool at the kitchen table, shoulders hunched, still deeply engrossed in the book, when Oscar arrived, startling her. She was not expecting him and had not heard him open the door.

"Oh! You're back? Is it that time already?" Ice asked

"Dad just dropped me off but he's gone straight back to work. He says it's OK because you're home and he's needed at the main office in Coventry. What are you reading? Have we got anything to eat? I'm starving." He reached up, opening the cupboard in his search for snacks. "Did you enjoy your day bunking off school? What did you do all day? Did you feel that quake again? Were you scared? It was cool. We were on the playground and loads of people screamed."

Oscar sat down on the opposite side of the table, opening a packet of chocolate digestive biscuits and taking out three. He offered one to Ice who shook her head.

"Yes, of course I felt it! I'm not sure I want any more of them though. It actually is getting a bit less fun now and I'd really like to know what's causing them," she replied.

"They're caused by the earth moving," Oscar sniggered.

"Yes. Thanks for that very useful information! You know what I mean!" Ice said, rolling her eyes.

"Can I see?" Oscar reached towards the book which was open in front of her. "Hey that's here! Depton. When did you get this?" he asked. "Ice! Did you go out? You weren't allowed!"

Ice sighed. "I wanted to find something out and I needed that book. Are you going to tell Dad?"

Oscar paused, seeming to consider his response before answering, "No, I'm not a 'snitch'. But only if you make me some coffee and tell me what you're finding out. Is it about the earthquakes?"

He wasn't allowed to drink coffee, but Ice considered it a small price to pay, as long as the evidence was gone before her dad returned. She glanced at her phone. They had a couple of hours still. Ice rose and filled the kettle. She placed a teaspoon of the crumbly, brown powder in each of two cups and added half a spoon of sugar.

"See that creature on the front... the 'shadeling' it's called?"

Oscar flipped the book over and stared at the artist's impression. He stabbed his finger at the creature's head.

"This one?"

"No, some other creature on the front cover!" Ice raised her voice slightly in frustration. It was hard not to give sarcastic replies to nine-year-old boys.

"OK, so what about it?"

"It's a local myth, I'm interested in."

Oscar pursed his mouth and made his eyes into slits, staring at her and showing Ice that he knew she was holding back.

"Alright, so I think they're not just myths!" she added with a brief laugh to cover the silliness of the idea. Oscar's response was a drawn out, "Cool!" and then, "What, like they're real? I wouldn't be surprised. There's all kinds of stuff like that!"

She didn't know how she had expected him to react but supposed she shouldn't have been surprised that someone who spent his life in virtual worlds wouldn't be bothered with distinctions between fantasy and reality. It was a sort of relief to have shared it with someone and not be totally ridiculed – even if it was only her fanciful younger brother.

"Yeah, well, maybe," she added, stirring his coffee and placing it on the table in front of him. She brought her own coffee over and retook her seat. Oscar read in his best film trailer voice, some of the titles of the chapters. He laughed out loud and laid special emphasis on the 'demonic cow'. He had to put his fingers up to represent horns on his head and cross his eyes, 'mooing' madly before sliding the book back across to Ice, who grinned too. She was grateful to him for adding his humorous spin on things and then, for a moment, the pair of them sat in silence, sipping their coffee on either side of the table. It made a change not seeing Oscar transfixed by his phone screen. Ice, as usual, was outwardly impassive, though a multitude of worrying thoughts were competing for her attention. The shadelings, of course... and then she wished she had not made such a bad start at school. What would the others be like tomorrow? It made her light-headed thinking about the incident in the dining hall. She wished her mother would respond to her texts. And always, in the background was the weather. It was impossible to ignore. And the earthquakes? At least they were things she could talk to her dad about and she intended to ask him that evening.

"Ice, have you heard from Mum?" Oscar's question cut across Ice's thoughts, taking her by surprise as though he had been reading her mind.

"Well, no – I've sent her a few texts but I haven't had a reply yet. Maybe there's a problem with the international connection. She should download the right app."

"Don't you ever miss her?" he asked, glancing quickly down into his coffee cup to mask any emotion.

"No! Yes… I don't know. I'm sort of used to it. Why are you asking this now?"

"I don't get it," Oscar replied, looking back at her. "Why have kids and then spend all your time away? Not even a text message!" He gave a dry laugh but the corners of his mouth wavered a little and Ice could tell it was a painful subject.

And that was the thing. Their mother was amazing – clever and good at her job, but she was away an awful lot. There was always a business trip to somewhere – they were used to that. Usually she would check in with them every day or two. Sometimes she couldn't because of the local conditions, so they had learned to be patient. But it did seem rather a long time since she had made contact.

When her job had first started taking her away, they had coped well enough. As it became more frequent and for longer amounts of time, it began to take its toll on a 6-year-old Oscar. Then the crying and the bed-wetting had started. Ice had done her best, reading him stories, or changing and washing the sheets secretly so that Dad didn't find out. Their father had made an effort to fill the gap, carrying on as though everything was normal, but he was also working more hours than ever and seemed tired and frazzled too. Eventually, Oscar found his way to cope through plunging himself into technology. To outside observers, Ice handled it

44

in her normal cold, detached manner – 'Ice by nature' and all that – as though it hadn't affected her.

"It's because I remembered she used to tell me stories about that magic kitten," Oscar picked up the thread again, glancing at the front of Ice's book. "She said she was going to write them one day and get them published…"

Ice tried to picture her mother sitting by Oscar's bed, relating one of these tales. She was slightly dismayed that she could not form a very clear image, though she was sure that what Oscar was saying was right. She looked at him for a moment and nodded slowly, taking another sip of coffee.

"I've got an idea," Ice stated. "Come with me."

Chapter 7
Suspicions

"Wow! This is old!" Oscar said it with a certain degree of admiration as he watched Ice boot up the computer in her bedroom.

"It works," Ice retorted, curtly. She slid the seat over slightly so that he could see the screen as it came to life with its ancient start-up jingle.

Ice rolled the mouse on the table, making the little arrow of a cursor move across the blue background. At the bottom left, she clicked an icon and opened the file explorer. Immediately a window popped up with an array of folders Ice had not bothered to look at before.

"I thought that if she had written anything down, it might be on here still," she explained to Oscar. There were a lot of folders with uninteresting work-related titles, but nothing that was obviously to do with children's stories.

"But maybe not," she said and sat back, taking in a deep breath and puffing it out in frustration.

"Move over, I'll have a look." Oscar nudged her aside off the chair and appropriated the mouse. He whipped the cursor over to the start icon again and this time opened a search window, typing in 'kitten'. This resulted in a list of web suggestions for 'kittens for sale', but also several files and a document.

"Hah! What's that?" Oscar opened it up and turned to Ice, delighted at his success. She raised her eyebrows as a response and read the document title, 'The Magic Kitten'.

"Oh my goodness! She did write it down! Wow! I didn't really think that we'd find anything. That's brilliant – well done!"

"Yeah well…" Oscar gave a 'jazz hands' flourish as an acknowledgement of his IT skills.

"All right, Cocky!" she smiled, "Enjoy!" and she left him to reminisce, happy to be reliving his favourite old bedtime story.

Ice returned downstairs to hide the evidence of her transgressions: the book and the coffee cups were out of sight by the time their father walked through the door. She told him that everyone was fine and that Oscar was upstairs. He accepted Ice's offer to make dinner but stayed in the kitchen, reading through work papers, while she stripped the plastic wrapper from the packet of sausages and shook them into a baking tray. When her mother was home, they were practically vegetarians but these days they ate what they could get. Shops didn't stock half the things they used to. It was funny how fads disappeared when food started to become scarce. The sight of the soft, meaty, pink objects still slightly turned Ice's stomach.

Her dad looked hassled. His dark hair, which Ice noticed was really starting to show strands of grey, had been allowed to grow longer than his usual short cut. It was unkempt as though it had been blown by the wind, and still a bit damp from outside. He frowned unconsciously and she could see the little muscles of his jaw flexing as he read. Lines on his face made him look older. Honestly, he had been huge fun, Ice remembered. She didn't blame him, but she missed his ridiculous sense of humour and the daddish teasing she and Oscar got. She remembered her brother's hysterical laughter as their dad would 'magically' pull a napkin from his nostril or walk round the room, making a squeaking noise like one of his legs needed oiling.

"Dad, those earthquakes are odd, aren't they?" she ventured, using the potato preparation as an excuse not to look at him directly. He glanced up, taking a second to refocus his attention.

"I suppose so, but like you said before, they do happen. I'm sure that both were just part of the same tectonic shift and that's it now. We probably won't get any more. You don't need to be frightened. Were you?"

"I w... wasn't really," she lied, stammering slightly and giving it away. "I was just... wondering what caused them. It's not... anything to do with your work, is it?" Ice could feel the fizzing sensation in her head as she asked this question. She was also a little too hot and her hair was tickling her face in an annoying manner. She removed an elastic hair tie from her wrist and swept her hair back so that it didn't interfere with her suddenly important job of scrubbing and slicing the potatoes.

"No. Nothing!" he answered, rather too snappily. "There's no proven link between this type of extraction and earthquakes. You shouldn't believe everything you see online, Ice."

"No, I wasn't." She bit her lip and let the subject drop. She was dismayed to realise that her father was lying. He rarely did that – unless it was something innocent like a birthday surprise. But that was the old father. Nowadays he just said very little about anything. She knew she had stepped into dodgy territory asking about the fracking and the earthquakes, but his reaction had been odd and now she couldn't stop herself getting in even deeper.

"Oscar asked about Mum."

There were those muscles again as he clenched his jaw. Ice carried on, reckless now.

"He misses her when she's away. I found him some of her old stories on the PC. He wanted to know if I'd heard from her – which I haven't for… since Saturday. Since we left London. Have you?" She was using Oscar as a foil, she knew, but then she added, almost as an indistinct mumble, "When should we start to get worried?"

For a moment, Ice wondered if her father was going to lose his temper. He gazed at her. She could see that his evening stubble was beginning to show as a dark shadow on his face, which had gone pale apart from a slight reddening over each cheek. Ice abandoned the potatoes and faced him, returning his stare openly. She was hiding her dismay but mentally daring him to say something so that she could confirm that he was a liar. It seemed longer, but it was a few seconds of intensity before he closed his eyes, sighed deeply and without opening them, replied, "Ice. I'm sure there's no need to worry. It's probably just that she's really busy, or there's no connection or something. She'll call or text. She always does, doesn't she?"

Ice waited. Sometimes it was better to force people to speak by an awkward silence. He leant his chin on his fist and glanced round the kitchen as though he would find some clues there.

"You know she really doesn't like to leave you or Oscar," he carried on. "It's just that this has been a very busy couple of years. When this is all sorted out," he waved at the paperwork in front of him, "things will get back to normal a bit."

Ice's heart sank. Her father was giving her the answers he thought she wanted to hear, but something was not right. It wasn't so much what he said, but the sense of something being held back. Her father was lying by omission – not telling her everything. She turned back quickly to the dinner she was preparing, so as not to show the devastation she was feeling. The knife that she was using on the potatoes slipped and she felt the sharp blade slice through the index finger on her left hand. Ice watched, transfixed as the blood spilled out, mingling pale red with the white, starchy flesh of the vegetables. She felt numb and unable to move. She knew her father was hiding something. Her head spun with the thought of it. What wasn't he telling her? Why? Ice felt like all her childhood trust in her father had just trickled out of her, like the blood from her finger which she watched disappear down the plughole of the sink as she turned on the tap.

Chapter 8
Friends and Enemies

Some silences are the comfortable kind where there's no need to fill space with conversation. This morning was not one of those. Ice could hardly bring herself to look at her father and refused his offer of a lift asking if it was OK if she rode instead as there was a lot of traffic this morning and being stuck in the car would make her feel ill. Oscar also seemed unusually subdued, staring at his bowl of cereal instead of his phone screen. It was still only half-finished by the time he left for school and Ice wondered if it had been a good idea finding the old magic kitten stories on the computer; she hadn't intended to unsettle him about their mother.

She had lied about her reasons for going on the bike. It was a deeply lonely, miserable journey through the heavy drizzle till she reached the school gate. There, she simply stopped motionless, unresponsive to the rainwater that had soaked her hair and was beginning to trickle in tiny rivulets into her eyes and down her cheeks. She felt hardly able to move, nor care. She was sure the day was going to be hideous but her anxiety about Monday's incident had been stripped away by her dismay at her father's response last night. Also gone was any level of energy or excitement she had previously felt. Pupils buzzed past, some jostling her as they went. She did not notice. Nor was she aware of those that were looking at her and pointing her out to their companions as 'the Girl who Smacked the Boy with a Dinner Tray'. The school entrance cleared remarkably quickly, leaving Ice as a solitary figure staring blankly after the punctual students. Dark laurel bushes lined the main walkway to the doors, gathering the precipitation and funnelling it through the leaves into a succession of miniature waterfalls on to the path. There was a stirring, shimmering movement within the branches and a dozen pairs of glowing yellow-green eyes were turned towards Ice as though waiting for her next move. Ice was aware that the shadelings had accompanied her entire journey from home, flowing in and out of the shadows, always keeping their distance, always maintaining their pursuit. She now watched them as they emerged, making their distinctive creaking sounds and sliding like fluid from the dark cover of the leaves, spilling out across the path. Tiny limbs seemed not entirely to contact the ground, though with movements that were something like the scampering of monkeys, something like the undulations of sea serpents, they disappeared into the school building within a few moments. Expressionless, and proceeding as though drugged, Ice followed.

It seemed to her that her fellow pupils were wary and embarrassed when she arrived, slightly late, into the form room. Mr Ward glanced up, not acknowledging her in any other way. Mia gave her a brief, reserved smile but did not wave her over and Ice sat down instead in the empty seat nearest the open door and stared down the corridor. She barely heard Mr Ward's voice as he ran through the register and she observed, dully and without reaction, the behaviour of the shadelings when they flickered into view from time to time unveiling themselves from the gloomy recesses around the class.

"Isis, may I have a word?" Mr Ward using her full name commanded her attention.

Registration was over; the brasher pupils were pushing their way out of the form room already. Some pulled faces to show that they knew Ice was in trouble and were glad it wasn't them. Mia glanced at her sympathetically but quickly left to go to her first lesson.

"You've gotten yourself in a bit of bother, it appears," he said to her when the room had emptied. Ice knew it was true but Monday's incident seemed like ancient history and she found she could no longer drum up a suitable response.

"You need to report to the head," he continued. Ice nodded and stood. Mr Ward didn't appear cross – he'd probably seen all sorts in his long teaching career.

"Look, Isis – you made a mistake, but this doesn't mean it has to go downhill from now on. If you keep out of trouble, you can still do well here."

Ice was hearing his words; she could see that he was making an effort to give her something positive to hold on to but she was unable to feel the impact. Whatever they had in store for her felt irrelevant.

"Thank you," Ice answered without expression and made her way to the head's office.

She knocked on the door and was summoned in. The head was at her desk and a boy was seated on one of the office chairs. Ice was slightly surprised to recognise that it was Joe. She could see the slight pink mark of the skin on his left cheek where she had hit him with the tray, although there was no terrible bruise as she had anticipated. Joe averted his gaze when he saw her, but not so quickly that she did not note the reddened rims of his eyes. It shocked Ice to think that he might have been crying. Mrs Pearce, the head, was the towering presence in the room and Joe seemed smaller, younger and more vulnerable in comparison.

"Sit down, please," Mrs Pearce instructed her. Ice complied without a word. Behind Mrs Pearce, a shadeling was making its way across the top of the bookcase.

"You have both caused me a lot of trouble as you well know. I have had to calm two sets of parents and neither of you is blameless in this matter. Isis – you are new to this school and I don't know what kind of rules they had at your previous school, but we cannot and will not accept violent behaviour of any sort here. In addition to your exclusion yesterday and being put on report, I have been asked that you write a formal letter of apology to Joe. I can tell you that it took a lot of diplomacy on my part to prevent Mrs Ross from taking it to the police."

At this point, Joe gave Ice a quick, surreptitious glance. He seemed more embarrassed than triumphant.

"But you, Joe are not innocent. I was on the phone to Nathan's mother for over an hour yesterday and I assured her that the bullying was going to stop once and for all. How dare you victimise anyone in this school, particularly after our anti-bullying assembly? For the rest of the half term you and the other boys who were involved are to take your lunch in the supervision room, and I do not want to hear of any other incidents of bullying of Nathan or anyone else. I hope you understand."

She was interrupted by a knock on the door. Ice recognised the young, mousy-haired woman as one of the office staff from her first day. The head followed her out of the room, leaving the two of them alone. Through the open door, Ice could just see them talking behind the glass partition of the main office. There was an obvious exchange of serious information and Mrs Pearce's expression became quite grave. She nodded and appeared to thank the secretary before adding something and returning to her own office with a new, concerned look on her face. Ice and Joe were dismissed without any further reprimands. As they left, Joe looked like he was on the brink of saying something to Ice but then shook his head and walked quickly in the other direction.

At lunchtime, Ice did not try to seek out Mia or Daniel. She assumed that they would think she was some kind of freak by now. Instead she found a concrete bench, partly sheltered from the rain by an overhanging balcony and in an out-of-the-way part of the school, where she sat hungry and not entirely alone because of the shadelings that were becoming ever more active and obvious. Even if she hadn't been in a state of numb misery, the shadelings would no longer have filled her with that initial feeling of dread. Ice had begun to accept their presence and the fact that others could not see them. She remembered Nathan's descriptive hand gestures in her room the other night. Shadelings all around outside. This is what he had meant.

"Aren't you going to have any lunch?" the voice came from one of the open windows of the building next to her. "Do you want this?"

One skinny arm was stretched awkwardly through the gap at the top of the window, proffering her an apple. It seemed like a peace gesture. Perhaps the fact that they had both been in trouble had given them a 'common enemy' as far as Joe was concerned. Ice suppressed a glimmer of gratitude to the boy whom she had earlier despised. She wanted to be angry still. Nevertheless she would be glad to be able to put that incident behind her. Not so long ago it would have been an enormous relief. She wished now that it was the only thing weighing on her mind.

"Thanks," she mumbled cautiously, taking the apple from him.

"No problem," Joe replied. An adult from inside called his name and he and disappeared back into the form room while she nibbled disconsolately at the piece of fruit.

"Save that." Ice heard a voice just as she was finishing her apple and wondering what to do with the core.

"We know someone who would like a bit of apple," Daniel continued.

Ice looked up, slightly confused. Mia was there too. She sat down next to Ice on the concrete bench.

"Where were you? I thought you might join us. Didn't you want to revisit the scene of your crime?" She gave a wry smile. Ice winced but she could see the pair of them were not going to treat her like a psychopath and that was good.

"Did you hear about BOB?" Daniel took up the unspoken thread of the conversation.

"What?" she asked.

"He's missing!"

At this point the two newcomers noticed Joe who had returned to the window and had his face pressed to the glass listening in to their conversation. The adult who had called him earlier could not be seen.

"This is your fault!" Daniel stated, pointing directly at the older boy.

"What? Hey! I didn't do anything to him!" Joe replied. He looked offended, but Ice could detect a surge of emotion. Guilt, perhaps? She wasn't sure. Perhaps it was just a habit. Some people were quick to deny responsibility, whatever they were accused of.

"Do you think he'd have run off if you hadn't subjected him to continuous teasing and bullying?" Daniel answered, the pitch of his voice rising slightly. Anger, and the fact that Joe was securely incarcerated with a wall between them, gave Daniel the bravado to confront him properly for the first time. Ice was as surprised as she always was when other people expressed their feelings so openly.

Joe paused. The window could only open part of the way and the expression on his face was masked by the reflection from outside. Ice wondered how he was going to justify his actions. His answer was a typical response, she was sad to note.

"We were only teasing him a bit. It was a joke!"

"Oh come on!" said Mia, joining in. "That's what bullies always say. Do you really think Bob found it funny? Did you never notice how uncomfortable he was? What did you think he felt like surrounded by people twice his size?"

"Nathan," Ice said.

The three of them turned to her, puzzled at her interjection.

"His name's Nathan. I met him on Monday. His mum brought him to our house. What do you mean, he's 'run off'? When? Have they told the police?"

"I don't know," Mia added, glowering in Joe's direction, 'probably he's hiding somewhere because he's scared to death to come to school and have to put up with you and your idiot mates!"

"OK, look, I get it!" Joe replied, rubbing his cheek where Ice had hit him. "Your friend here made that point pretty clearly two days ago. You disapprove. Maybe we should've noticed that the little guy wasn't having a good time, but you know how it is. You get kind of caught up in the moment and it's funny. Why did he have to be so weird and make those sounds? You must admit that's not normal. I didn't think he'd go and do something stupid like running away or whatever."

"You didn't think, sums it up really," Daniel came back at him. "People like you never do think about the harm you're doing. And as for not normal – what's normal? You and your fellow morons? Getting your kicks from tormenting little kids?"

Joe rolled his eyes as his only defence and disappeared back in to the gloom of the form room.

"Come on, let's go. Bring your apple core," Daniel said, pointing at the bit Ice was still holding. "There are better things to do than give people like him our time. I think you'll like this."

She followed them both to a part of the school she had not seen yet. They led through a paved courtyard and a covered walkway out into an open space that was a grassy fenced area.

"Meet Peaches and Cream."

Mia and Daniel seemed amused and proud to introduce Ice to two chunky pygmy goats that trotted over to the fence as soon as they noticed the humans. The rain had slowed to a soft mizzle and Ice was charmed to have her offering of the apple core greedily snaffled by one of the little animals. Mia, not wanting to play favourites, brought out some bits of celery that she had saved from the canteen salad.

"These guys are cool aren't they? Animals always make things feel a bit better," she said.

"They didn't tell me the school had goats," Ice replied, nodding.

"Really? They're a bit famous. They've got their own social media page. Bob... um... Nathan... was always here," Daniel told her. "I think they let him help out – like a special responsibility or something. When the earthquake happened, he ran here. I don't know if he was comforting the goats or if they were comforting him. I don't think much fazes these sturdy little chaps, though."

"It fazes me. It would be nice if we didn't have to put up with it," Mia retorted. "I wish they'd stop fracking the hell out of our countryside!"

Ice was suddenly alert. The word had grabbed her attention. She felt a surge of associated guilt and embarrassment that they were talking about her father's company.

"Do you think it's a problem? I thought the new system was safer." She leaned over the smooth wooden top of the fence and rubbed the coarse fur between the little horns on Peaches' head. It was a useful distraction to avoid giving away her particular interest in Mia's answer. The goats were keen to see if the children had brought any more food and were jostling each other for best position.

"Are you kidding?" Mia answered. Daniel looked up too, replying, "Yes," with a brief cynical snort of laughter. "Don't you know what's going on round here?"

Ice didn't like deceiving them, but she shook her head not wanting to give away her connection to somebody in the business.

"It's awful," Mia went on. "All this stuff is because of the fracking. All these earthquakes and the disgusting smell in the water."

"And then there's the pollution," Daniel continued. "We had a really great wildlife area that was completely destroyed by the chemicals they used. It was a disaster. Loads of fish and birds died. Everybody knew that it was because of the fracking company, but nobody did anything. They just got away with it. And it's all so we can continue our ridiculous addiction to fossil fuels which we should have stopped using ages ago. Look at this!" He waved his hands at the weather. "It's not normal, is it? We know we've changed our climate. It's not supposed to be raining for weeks on end. My nan's house is half under water and she's had to move in with us. But they won't listen to us. My mum's a town councillor and they objected to the fracking, but she says the county council have some kind of deal with the company and it all went ahead anyway. It's all corrupt!"

He paused, seeming to become aware that both girls were looking at him.

"Sorry!" he laughed. "I know I'm having a bit of a rant! It just makes me cross that these people can come over here and do these things and there's nothing that we can do to stop them."

Ice was acutely aware that her father would be one of 'these people' that Daniel was talking about. She didn't like the reminder that he was involved in something other people thought of as wrong. She had always thought of him as one of the 'good guys'. Now, last night's conversation had planted a seed of mistrust in her mind. And Daniel's speech had added the horrible thought that the company her father worked for was a corrupt, dangerous organisation. With a sudden pang of paranoia, Ice wondered whether her mother's lack of contact was in any way connected to it.

Chapter 9
Rising Waters

It was raining in ridiculous amounts when Ice left school that afternoon. Giving up on thoughts of trying to stay out of it or keep dry, instead she embraced the uncompromising soaking she would get on the way home. If the water was going to drench her, then at least she would feel it fully. Humans were sentient beings – cold, wet, hungry – these were all reminders that you were still alive! Nathan was her concern, though. The idea that something might have happened to him, gave her a sick feeling. He seemed to her like an innocent, and furthermore, she felt a shared connection with him through the shadelings. Ice wanted to know where Nathan was and to believe that he was safe, but she imagined him somewhere alone and frightened.

She left hurriedly, heading towards the town. Her plan was mainly to follow the bounding, scampering shapes of the shadelings who were still with her constantly but now seemed to be taking a lead rather than just accompanying her. They appeared utterly unaffected by the water. Though their 'skin' shimmered constantly, there was no indication that they were even touched by the rain: nothing splashed nor dripped from them as they ran before her. She wasn't really surprised. The shadelings, she decided, didn't fully occupy the world of concrete things, but seemed to flicker between it and their own unknown domain.

"Ice wait!"

She heard the voice through the drumming of the downpour and, turning, annoyed at having to stop, saw that it was Joe. Ice frowned slightly. She waited for him to catch up but did not speak. The shadelings hovered just ahead of her, invisible to him, of course.

"Where are you going in this?" Joe demanded. She peered at him, squinting and vainly wiping away the water that was running into her eyes. Ice could not see why it was of interest to Joe where she was going nor what she was doing. She was glad that he seemed to have forgiven her for the dinner tray incident, but she was still cross that there was any forgiving to be done. She didn't think that he fully got it, yet. How could people like him know what it was like for those on the receiving end of the so-called fun? Ice turned back towards town.

"Hey!" Joe shouted. "I wanted to talk to you. Stop! Can't we get out of this? I can hardly hear myself."

Ice slowed down but did not stop. She could see that Joe had come alongside and was staring at her strangely. He had his coat hood up but it was ineffectual against the downpour.

"I want to look for Nathan," she said, and suspected immediately from Joe's facial expression, that it sounded like an odd thing to do. Perhaps he was thinking that she would have no idea where to start. But then Joe couldn't see the shadelings who had an air of insistence about them now and almost seemed to be impatient for her to follow. She rode off and Joe had to break into a jog to keep up.

Even though it was difficult to see through the torrents of water, Ice reached the Victorian stone bridge that crossed the river. The car drivers were nicely dry inside their vehicles, yet the rain spurred them on, as if it were triggering an instinct to run for home. They apparently did not care about the plumes of spray they were throwing up over the two youngsters. Ice leaned her bike against the bridge wall. She held on to one of the thick pillars and looked over the edge. Weeks of rain had turned the once placid waterway into a churning, white surge that rose in foaming peaks as it met the resistance of the stonework below. In drier times, canoeists had paddled through the arches, but these were now completely obliterated by the flooding waters which were still rising and threatening to submerge the bridge and everything on or around it.

When Ice looked up from the waves, she became aware that they were not the only people peering hopelessly over the bridge.

"Ice!" shouted Mrs Bennett as they recognised each other simultaneously. She looked awful. Ice thought she may have been crying but it was impossible to tell in the pouring rain. "Have you seen him?" Ice could barely hear the question above the noise of the crashing waters. There was desperation in Mrs Bennett's face and Ice wished she could have had a more comforting response. She shook her head.

"If he's fallen in there, he'd never survive!" Mrs Bennett yelled, indicating the treacherous waves below.

"Mrs Bennett – we're looking for him!" Joe was bending down and yelling so that he could make himself heard. "I'm sorry – I think this is all my fault!"

Mrs Bennett frowned at the boy through the streaming water. Ice was surprised at Joe's sudden admission of guilt.

"Who are you?" Nathan's mother demanded.

"Joe. I... we... BOB, I mean Nathan is at our school. I'm one of the ones who was… teasing him. I'm really sorry!" He hunched his shoulders and looked like he was trying to disappear into his hood.

Mrs Bennett looked from Joe to Ice and back again as if piecing together an old story. She shook her head.

"That's got nothing to do with this! He was after those damned imaginary, stupid animals of his. One minute he was babbling about the creatures - 'creakers' he calls them – and then he was off out. I heard the front door bang but by the time I got outside I couldn't see where he had gone!"

It was bizarre that Nathan's mother was talking about the 'creakers' in this way, oblivious to the fact that not more than a foot away, several of them were watching her intently. If she could have heard them, she would have known that the name wasn't his childish pronunciation of the word 'creature' but because of the creaking sounds they constantly made as they 'chattered' to each other.

"Mrs Bennett – we're going to keep looking along the river where we can!" shouted Ice. "Have you told the police? Shouldn't you go home? He'll probably turn up and you'll need to be there." She wasn't sure she believed her own words, but she did not yet have the sense that Nathan was lost forever. She still had the peculiar impression that the shadelings were telling her something and that Nathan was a part of it.

When Ice hurried on across the road and downstream, Joe hesitated and she was aware that he was saying something to Mrs Bennett before he left. As he caught up with her again, he grabbed her by the sodden wet sleeve of her coat and pulled her further from the water's edge which was lapping the cycle path and completely covering it in some places. Joe dragged Ice up the slippery bank beside the path.

"Ice – I can't see much point in this!" he yelled into her face. "You're actually putting yourself at risk and we have no idea where Nathan is!"

Ice glowered at him and shook him off. She could see that the shadelings were waiting for her further downstream.

There were now maybe twenty or thirty little black faces turned towards her and what looked like an array of glowing eyes all focussed in her direction. The way ahead, though, was already hidden beneath the murky, brown embrace of the flood water and though she wanted to follow, there was no longer a way through without risking being swept away. Ice stopped trying to resist and nodded, beginning to scramble up the bank, pulling her bike up on to the road above.

"OK, you're right," she gasped. "We need to go home or they'll start sending out people to look for us!"

The pair of them trudged with some effort and in silence along the road, ignoring the rush of traffic next to them. It was too hard to speak above the roar of the cars and the water combined. Ice realised that following the shadelings had taken her away from the familiar parts of Depton. She might have needed the map on her phone, without recognising soon that they were on the main route between her house and the school. Eventually Joe put out a hand to stop her and indicated that they had reached his turn off for home. He leaned in close to shout in her ear.

"They'll find him, Ice. I'm sure they will. Maybe we can look more tomorrow if this stops, yeah? I still feel like it's my fault." Ice could tell that he wasn't exactly lying, but he wasn't completely convinced by his own admission. She stared at him for a moment. He no longer looked anything like the arrogant bully she encountered on Monday. Inside the hood she could see a pinched, pale face framed by the dark dripping spikes of hair which the rain had plastered to his cheeks and forehead.

"OK," she said, briefly. Ice was starting to shiver – not just from cold and the rain that had soaked through her coat – and she set off in the direction of home. Without needing to look back, she knew that Joe had stood for a few seconds, watching her hurried departure, before he turned to continue up the side road to his house.

Chapter 10
Evidence

Ice had expected a bit of a reprimand from her father when she got home. She was late and if he had arrived before her, he would have started to worry. What she didn't expect was to find a marked police car on the drive waiting for her. Bracing herself for the questioning and explanation that she was sure to face, she let herself in through the front door and took off her sopping wet coat to hang it, dripping in the hallway.

She found nobody in the kitchen but Buddy who had mysteriously been shut in and was frantically snuffling at the bottom of the door. However, the living room was full of people and all turned to face her when she entered, though her father, she noticed, quickly returned his gaze to the floor. He looked forlorn. It was odd. Lately he had seemed frazzled, but now he sat slumped with his elbows resting on his knees, hands hanging loosely. It was like some of the air had been let out of him. A woman spoke to Ice. She was wearing the black padded jacket and utility belt which identified her as the police. An old-fashioned walkie-talkie was clipped to her left shoulder and some keys and a small torch hung from the right. Ice noticed she had removed her police hat and it was on the sofa making a damp patch. The woman held something in a plastic wallet. She introduced herself as PC Owens.

Ice's father looked up and she caught his eye. His facial expression was strange – like that of someone who had just accidentally walked into something solid and was still a bit dazed but just beginning to realise that it hurt.

"The officers have some news," he said, quietly. Ice looked round the room, identifying the uniformed male as the other officer. Oscar was there too, sitting on the edge of one of the old chairs. He gave Ice an odd look. He had his lips pursed tightly and was frowning. He gave an abrupt shake of his head. Ice could feel the rising swell of anxiety. She did not want to know what the officers had to say, but she turned her gaze back to her father, saying nothing and waiting for him to go on.

"They've found something. It doesn't make sense." he said. Ice frowned. What? Had they found Nathan? Were her instincts wrong and he had not survived after all? It seemed a bizarre way to tell her: 'Something'? What thing? Had something dreadful happened to him?

"Is it Nathan?" She asked. "What happened? Where did you find him...?"

"Er... no. Not that. Isis – is it...?" The female police officer glanced at Ice's dad, who nodded, miserably, for her to continue and dropped his head into his hands. "We found something... this was handed in to your dad's company. He contacted us." She held out a plastic wallet for Ice to see. Inside was an object that might have been pulled out of some mud. It was one of those ID badges attached to a lanyard that was probably once green but was now a mottled, dirty brown. Someone had recently wiped the surface of the badge to see the photograph that was in the top left corner, next to the person's name. Beneath that was a logo: Konnara Resources. It was her parents' company. It was her mother's ID badge. Ice stared at it. 'Be ice,' she commanded herself, using her old mantra, though she had to shove her hands into her pockets to stop them trembling. Without looking up, she asked, "What does this mean? Who found this? Where?"

"We're not sure of all the details, yet, but it seems it was washed away with the floods and it caught on one of the bushes by someone's house. A member of the public picked it up thinking it might be important. The floods are dangerous. People have... well you know. It's not safe to take risks." Owens was talking quietly and sympathetically. It annoyed Ice. She wasn't a small child or a frightened animal. "When the company contacted your dad, he called us. He was worried." Ice felt like she wanted to laugh. It sounded ridiculous. Her mum was in the states. Buddy was still shut in the kitchen and she could hear him giving his low bark and jumping up, trying to turn the handle.

"I was getting worried," her father said, almost imperceptibly. "She hasn't answered any of our texts. I called her phone..."

"She's fine!" said Oscar.

"Oscar..." Her dad started.

"I know how hard this must be. I'm so sorry, Mr Cooper," the officer was saying. "We will file this as a genuine missing person and start a proper search. Try not to worry. There could be a million explanations for..." her voice tailed off and then she picked it up on a different tack. "But... we have counselling services available if need be. Here are the contact details and the case number." She now seemed keen to leave, holding out a card as she stood up. Mutely, Ice's dad took it and walked with the unwelcome visitors to the door. Oscar, too got up. He pushed past all of them and ran upstairs. It was strange for him to be so stubborn. Ice herself, was struggling to process the information. What were they saying? Counselling? What for? Her mother was in the USA. She was with them two weeks ago. Why was her ID here? Had she come to Depton without telling anyone? Why would she do that? Why wouldn't she answer her phone?

She stood where they had all left her, in the middle of the living room. Her father had tried to talk to her. He had put his arm around her and told her that it didn't mean anything. The police were right. There could be all sorts of reasons… and then he had stopped. She gradually became aware that her father had gone out with the dog and that the room was now filled with the white noise of the weather. Tear-shaped, bright eyes still observed her from the dark recesses, but she was becoming so used to the presence of the shadelings that now she hardly cared. Slowly she made her way to her room and sat motionless on her bed. She pulled out her phone and tapped on her mother's number. The voice on the other end relayed the information that the phone was unavailable. Though Ice could still hear Oscar's fervent denial ringing in her ears, she felt unable to match his conviction that her mother was fine. As though someone had cut the strings that held her up, Ice allowed herself to slump on to her side, her feet still dangling over the edge of the bed, and she lay there staring at the blank wall where the shadow of the computer was cast by the streetlight shining through the window.

Oscar had been standing in her doorway for several minutes, observing her motionless form on the bed before she noticed that he was there. She sat up quickly.

"She's fine," he said again, from the doorway.

"Oscar…" Ice frowned. She was starting to be cross with him. What right did he have to be so certain? "I don't want to think anything bad has happened either, but you saw the ID badge, the same as I did. It was her photograph! She's not answering her phone."

"I don't know how her badge got there or why she's not texting but she's OK. I know it! She could have dropped that ID anytime. People do that you know. They lose stuff. It doesn't mean they've died in an accident!"

He should have been crying or shouting. That would have been easier to understand. His reactions were wrong. He almost seemed excited. Ice flopped back down on the bed.

"I don't know what to tell you, Oscar. This is just another bit of craziness to add to the last few days. Why isn't she replying to our texts and our calls?" Ice felt that the room was rocking, but this time she knew it was just her reaction to the news – not an earthquake. Things like this happened only to other people. She could feel the panic threatening to melt her icy reserve.

Oscar didn't reply. Instead, he stepped into her room and pushed the button for the computer screen, lighting it up with its distinctive blue glow. He jiggled the mouse and the blue screen changed to the old-fashioned desktop background. Their mum's computer had missed all the upgrades. Without a word, he pointed his finger at the screen and gave Ice a challenging stare.

"What? What am I supposed to be looking at?" Her voice was tetchy, but she sat up and looked at the screen where he was pointing. There were the files they had found the previous night – the ones her mother had made – but Oscar was pointing to an icon inside the window of an open file. It was labelled simply 'email'.

"Click on it," Oscar prompted, "go on!"

Ice sighed but she followed his instructions and it opened up a webpage from an online email account, asking for a password. Oscar leaned across her and typed in an email address and combination of letters and numbers.

"Oscar! This is mum's email!" Ice turned to him, demanding to know how he had the right address and password.

"It took a few goes," he replied, and gave a brief laugh and a shrug. "It wasn't so difficult. Maybe mum is very clever at her job, but her Internet use is a bit basic. She's got her email address saved in this file – and her password was kind of obvious. I did different ways round of our names and birthdays. I did it when you left me up here with the cat story. I think it took me about fifteen tries."

"Bloody hell, Oscar!" Ice stared at him with increased admiration. He could still surprise her.

"Yeah but look at the emails, Ice! There's some weird stuff in there. Like she was in this argument with some people in her company and she goes on about some of those things people have been saying on the telly. I don't understand what they're all about, but you should have a look." Oscar waved his hand at the screen as if giving Ice the freedom to go through all her mother's communications herself.

"OK. This is all very interesting, Oscar, and I'm very impressed at your hacking skills… but I still don't get what this has to do with anything. Of course she wrote to people about the work she did." Ice shrugged, but she had begun to catch some of his excitement.

"Look at the dates," Oscar said, quietly.

The emails were all listed in chronological order with the most recent at the top of the list. Ice stared at it, feeling her heart-rate quicken. The most recent email had been sent yesterday. Whatever the police thought, she had been alive then at least. So what was going on and why wasn't she in contact with them? Ice so wanted to agree with Oscar.

"You're right…" she said, turning and looking at him. "This is really important… but can you keep it to yourself – for just a little while? Don't tell Dad yet… er… just in case." It sounded a bit lame. Ice wanted to find a way to tell Oscar that their father should be kept out of the loop but she did not want her little brother to have to share her burden that she was scared he was hiding something from them. She made up some reason about Dad being cross with them for looking through their mum's stuff and they needed to be sure that they were really important first. It wasn't very convincing. Oscar frowned and complained, but he agreed to hold off until Ice said.

"See what you can find, quickly though, please," he said. "I want to tell Dad soon!"

Chapter 11
Konnara Resources

Their father had tried to be a comforting parent the night before but it was all a bit clumsy and unsuccessful. Ice had felt sorry for him. He was clearly suffering, but she had been unable to help. Oscar had glared at her with wide eyes, silently demanding that they tell their father what they found but she had subtly shaken her head and Oscar had kept quiet and sullen. Ice hated making him keep secrets. It was the last thing she wanted. Though she desperately needed to talk to someone, the feeling that her father was hiding something meant that it could not be him. Everything was a jumble, a cascade of thoughts flooding her mental space. The shadelings, Nathan, the tremors, the floods, her mother. She stepped out quickly before their dad returned from walking Buddy. For once it was not raining, and it was far too early for school, so she pedalled slowly, making the most of the change in the weather and prolonging the journey. She needed to think what to do.

It was clear to her that things were not as they seemed with the company that her father and mother worked for. She had read those emails late into the night and looked through all the documents on her mother's desktop. Ice could not comprehend a lot of the technical information in the messages, but she understood their tone. It was obvious that her mother was not happy with something she had discovered about the safety of the proposed fracturing operation, and she had increasingly tried to warn her superiors. There were official-looking documents about the water table and references to geological reports which gave percentage likelihoods of 'disruption' or 'seismic events'.

Earthquakes! Most disturbing however, was an exchange of emails her mother had saved that seemed to be between someone at the company and the leader of the County Council about obtaining permission to start drilling. Her mother had highlighted words and phrases which at first glance looked like just the normal jargon of business: 'remuneration', 'our mutual advantage', 'remain discreet on this matter' and so on. Though she was not sure what it all meant, Ice could tell enough to know that the highlighted words indicated secrecy and money – never a good combination. Ice had downloaded all the emails and documents on to an old-fashioned USB pen-drive – she had it now, in her coat pocket. She needed to share this with someone. She just didn't know who.

Before she realised it, she had made it to the school gate. A few pupils were arriving early. No shadelings were visible. With forty minutes to spare before registration, she found herself, unsurprisingly, at the goat enclosure. Though she knew she would have to speak to another human soon, the company of animals was always preferable. Ice regretted that she hadn't thought to bring them any treats, but she bent down and tore up some of the longer, greener grass that hadn't been trammelled into the mud outside their fence. Immediately the two came over, demonstrating the cheeky curiosity goats have when food is a probability.

"Where is she? And where is Nathan, eh?" Ice said to them, softly, holding the grass out and welcoming the quick, warm furriness of their mouths as they nibbled at her hands. She could imagine the young boy here, recently, talking in his matter-of-fact way to the creatures. "Did he tell you things, I wonder? Ice closed her eyes and breathed in the earthy smell of the little animals, reminded instantly of all the times her mother had taken her to the petting areas at zoos or visited farms with her as a child. She didn't know how long she had been standing there when she became aware of company and opened her eyes to find both Mia and Daniel standing next to her.

"Hello," Mia said, "Are you alright?"

"You were away with the fairies," Daniel added.

Ice shook her head.

Mia spoke again. "Is it about Nathan? We're worried too. There's a full-on manhunt out looking for him now. He's been gone for nearly 24 hours! It's horrible. I don't want to hear what's happened to him."

Ice nodded and then shook her head again.

"My mum's missing," she said bluntly.

Both friends gawped at Ice in wide-eyed silence and she realised how shocking this must have sounded to them.

"She was meant to be in the USA for work, but we don't know where she is. She was supposed to meet us at the house tomorrow and we've heard nothing from her for several days. She was in Dallas," she went on, "But they found her work ID here!"

"Ice, that's awful! Do you want to talk about it?" Mia asked. Ice nodded. It was odd but she did want to. Were Mia and Daniel becoming her friends? Would they think it was all a bit too freaky? They hadn't been put off before and maybe talking to them would help to put some of the disturbing thoughts, at least, in their place.

It turned out not to be such a long story, after all. Ice filled them in on the background and the unsettling events of the past night, though she avoided all mention of the shadelings. She showed them the USB pen-drive and asked, "So what do I do with this, now?"

Both children stared at the small, plastic object in silent amazement and then Mia put her arms around her.

"You've had a tough time!" she exclaimed. "Shouldn't you tell your dad, though? All this sounds way too much for you to deal with on your own."

"Maybe. But he's being all weird. When I told him that I hadn't heard from her, he brushed it off and I know he was lying to me. He's hiding something. Then he called the police in and now he's demanding a search," Ice replied, "but…" She hesitated for a moment, wondering how much to reveal, before ploughing on. "He works for that company. I didn't want to get him into trouble." She could not bring herself to tell them that she wasn't sure whether her dad was involved in something bad or not. Daniel, who had been quiet up to this point, suddenly roused himself.

"I know who we can take this to!"

"What do you mean? Who?" Mia queried.

"My mum. Don't you see? She's been fighting this operation for years. If anyone knows anything about it, she does. And she'll help, Ice! I know she will. You need an adult to talk to – well I'm offering you one!"

"Your mum?" And then Ice put the association together. She could see the family resemblance. Daniel King – of course – Anna King, his mum, the local town councillor she had seen on the news video. It was a good coincidence and Ice was relieved to grab on to the lifeline – to any thread of sanity offered.

"That's done, then. I'll wait for you after school and you can come round to mine. You too, Mia, if you like."

"Thank you so much!" Mia replied with sarcasm, but she linked arms with the pair of them and walked them towards the door. "Come on. We're going to be late. We'll talk later? Will you be OK till then, Ice?"

Ice nodded. The old mantra was true then. It did help to talk, apparently. She felt just a tiny bit more 'OK' than she had for a while.

After school, Daniel was as good as his word and was waiting for them both. His house was less than ten minutes' walk up the hill – the middle of a late Victorian terrace – well clear of the flood zone, Ice thought.

Mrs King was home when they arrived and met them in the hallway. Ice recognised her from the video: she had blond hair, like Daniel, who had already overtaken her in height, and she was rather young-looking to be his parent. She greeted Mia, whom she clearly knew well, and then Daniel introduced Ice. Before his mum could welcome her in, Daniel had already bombarded her with a potted version of Ice's story.

"You can help her, can't you, Mum? That's your sort of thing, isn't it? It's that company stuff – she's got information!" Mrs King looked slightly taken aback, but suggested that they go into the kitchen. Daniel could make them a cup of tea and she would get her laptop to have a look at the contents of Ice's pen-drive.

"Wow!" Mrs King exclaimed, when she had finished reading. "I didn't expect that! This is pretty damning stuff. Ice – I always knew that there was something dodgy going on with that company and the county council and it looks like your mum thought the same thing. She was building up evidence. These last documents are about the site here in Warwickshire. They show geologic reports that don't look good."

"Her mum's disappeared. She… they found her ID and…" Daniel interjected quietly but faded out before saying anything more, causing his mother to glance in Ice's direction, disturbed by that information. He went on, not giving her time to reply, "That's why we came to you. Her dad works for them. She needed to talk to someone who could help, that wasn't part of the company. What should she do, Mum?"

Anna King took in a deep breath, closed her eyes and exhaled slowly.

"I'm so sorry, Ice. You must be beside yourself with worry – but we do need to do the sensible thing, Daniel. She needs to tell her father, first of all, and then we should to turn this all over to the police and let them investigate." Mrs King sounded as though she had some reservations about her own advice but pressed on. "I want to show you something, too, though," she said. She typed into the laptop and opened up a video page. Turning it towards the children, she pointed to two men in suits being interviewed for the local news. They were standing at an outside location and the interview was hampered by the blustery weather. It was like a comedy sketch in which they were trying to come across as serious and convincing while they had to keep stopping their ties from being blown by the wind and fluttering up in front of their faces.

"That," said Mrs King, pointing at the man on the right, "Is the area manager for Konnara Resources, David Hunt, and that," indicating the other, "is Councillor Bennett."

"Bennett?" Ice asked. That name.

"Yes – Nathan's dad," Mia told her.

The children listened. The men were having an interview about the fracturing operation. It had just been given the go-ahead by the council and both men wore self-congratulatory smiles and were saying what a wonderful opportunity it was, creating jobs and boosting the economy. The interviewer asked how they would address the concerns of the local community, and could they reassure people that there would be no dangerous side-effects such as earthquakes or problems with the drinking water. Both men gave authoritative and dismissive responses. There was no danger at all. The whole operation had been fully risk-assessed and it was an ideal location. Stories from the USA were just scare-mongering and this was a completely different process to the ones that had caused concerns abroad. They looked forward to a time of prosperity, jobs, and reduced fuel costs for all. Lastly, the interviewer asked how the councillor responded to allegations that there had been 'pay-offs' by the company to speed up the process and obtain permission to begin drilling. Nothing untoward had gone on at all. Everything was by the book and, frankly, the councillor was disappointed that some people were grasping at straws to try to stand in the way of progress.

The video ended with the interviewer thanking them and turning back to camera with a general comment about the location. Ice's expression was closed, but her blood ran a little colder; she could tell that both of the men had been lying about nearly everything.

Chapter 12
Mistaken Identity

She stayed with the Kings for as long as she could. She really wasn't ready to face her father yet, even though she knew it was a bit cowardly of her and she felt a pang of guilt about leaving Oscar to do it alone; she hoped he would do his normal escape act of hood up, head down over his screen. Their father had learned by now that this was his way – he would surely just leave him alone. She checked her phone again, vainly hoping to have a text from her mother. Then she sent both her brother and her father a dishonest message about staying late for dinner and being back before dark. Normally, her dad would have questioned this. Only three days in school and already she was at someone's for dinner. But he was so distracted at the moment, she would probably get away with it.

It was at five o'clock that Ice received a phone call from her father, which she ignored, followed by a text which she didn't. It was demanding that she return at once. Though it was only a simple message, Ice caught the tone, experiencing a sudden quickening of her pulse. She said her 'Goodbyes' and left with Mia straight away. Mrs King kept the pen-drive and reassured the children that she would deal with it and the police, but with the promise that Ice would immediately tell her father everything. Heavy clouds had made the evening prematurely dark but below these, the setting sun was now just about visible on the horizon, casting a pale, yellow glow across the route home. The two girls walked, mainly in silence, Ice wheeling her bike, until Mia gave Ice a brief hug and told her it would be 'OK', as she turned to go up her road, leaving Ice to her thoughts and the last part of her journey. She did not feel like it was 'OK'.

Before she cycled off, she scanned the dark areas beneath the hedges and in the shadows of the doorways but could find no sign of the shadelings. She should have felt relieved but she did not. It had begun to seem like the shadelings had some intent – some important warning for her – and now their disappearance worried her. There were too many absences at the moment. They were so often indicators of worse things. Like the silence of birdsong because of the nearness of a predator; or the absence of buzzing insects due to their decline. She was so absorbed with this train of thought that the sudden sensation of a hand on her shoulder made her jump and back away quickly, nearly dropping her bike. Ice saw that it was Joe and scowled.

"Don't do that!" she shouted.

"Sorry!" he said, holding up his hands as though proving he had no weapons. "I called your name but you didn't seem to hear."

He needed to stop being there, Ice thought. And stop making like he was a good sort of person and trying to sort things out about Nathan.

"What do you want?" she asked him, the irritation obvious in her voice. "Why do you keep following me?"

Joe gave a snort of derision at this.

"I wasn't following you. I was out. There's nobody home and I've had my key taken off me." He shoved his hands in the pockets of his coat and hunched up his shoulders. Ice thought she heard him murmur, "I don't even want to be there, so it doesn't matter."

"Anyway – look!" he raised his voice, again and shoved a sopping, green object towards Ice.

"It's a hat," she muttered, blankly, but she knew what he was going to say next.

"Yes – it's a hat. Well done. It's his hat! Nathan's! I found it just now. Not by the river at all. It was by the gate to the Twelve Brothers field. And the thing is this – I go past that field all the time and it wasn't there before. I reckon Nathan was there really recently."

Joe was staring at her, his eyes glittering with excitement. He seemed so desperate to solve this, she wondered if he was grasping at straws. Nevertheless, it was true. She could picture Nathan in his green, woolly hat, and the one in Joe's hands, though soaked and muddy, was the same.

Ice felt her phone buzz in her pocket and pulled it out, quickly. There were three missed calls from her father and two from Oscar since she had last checked. The phone was reminding her to check her texts. She had missed them all. She sighed. Still feeling guilty that she had left her little brother to deal with their father without her, she turned away from Joe to read his last message.

"OK, just hang on a minute. I need to check this."

Joe stood, waiting impatiently as she opened Oscar's message:

> police found body! Where R u? Dad going to ID driving now when u home? Ice!!!!!

Ice's head spun and she thought she was going to topple sideways, bicycle and all, into the mud. She was vaguely aware of Joe's grip on her coat, steadying her as she let the bike drop. It didn't seem real. That message had come an hour ago. Adrenalin was like a sharp pain in the middle of her chest. She stared at the screen and then at Joe, vaguely aware of his puzzled face. Ice remembered that the last set of documents they had looked at on the pen-drive had been about this site. Had her mum been here? Was that when she had lost her ID? The thought of her brother and father driving to identify a body made her suddenly nauseous and she bent over, taking deep breaths. She felt the phone vibrate again in her hand and glanced down.

not mum. some old lady cos flood. come home.

Ice could hear herself laughing. The sound of it in her own ears was unhinged and distant. Oscar's text-speak gave his message a trivial quality that didn't fit with the weight of information he had just conveyed. A body had been found. Her dad had had to go and identify it – some poor old soul who had fallen foul of the floods. Could they not see it didn't fit her mother's description? She'd missed all this while she was at Daniel's house. Ice sensed Oscar's plea in the last part of his message – it was time to go home. Suddenly it felt imperative to share things with her father.

"Are you OK?" It was Joe, sounding disconcerted by her odd behaviour and her unexpected laughter. She'd almost forgotten he was there. Ice looked at her phone, then at the hat in Joe's hands and at his earnest expression.

"I'm fine. It's fine." Her voice was trembling. "Look, Joe, I think you're right, probably, but I can't do this now! You should tell someone about the hat – your parents. Tell the police. They'll need to do a search or something. He must be hiding, but…" She wasn't quite sure how to finish, nor what Joe expected from her; he looked dissatisfied. That wasn't her fault – they weren't supposed to be bonding over this or anything! When she thought of Nathan, she felt sure he would be found somewhere, safe, soon. Maybe. But he wasn't the only one missing and she needed to go home right now. She was irritated by Joe's sombre stare and his disappointment.

"Oh what?" she shouted at him. "What do you want me to do?"

"I don't want you to do anything," he replied coldly, still watching her. He looked eerie in the fading light and she was overly aware of his eyes, large pupils dark against the paleness of his face. "You wanted to find Nathan, remember?" he went on. "You nearly went into the river, remember?"

That was an exaggeration. She picked up her bicycle and began to pedal off.

"Fine!" he shouted after her. "Off you go! I'll find him myself!"

Chapter 13
The Twelve Brothers

Ice found all the house lights still off apart from in the kitchen where both her brother and father were sitting at the table. They looked like they had been talking for some time. Buddy was curled up in his bed in the corner of the room. He was the first to notice Ice and jumped up, wiggling his greeting as boxers do. Oscar was next.

"There you are!" he said, announcing the obvious. "We've been waiting for you – why did you ignore all our calls? Did you get my messages?"

"Um. Yes," she lied hesitantly. She was rubbish at it. "My phone was nearly out of battery so I had it turned off. I only just got them." Ice moved on quickly. "It's a bit crazy, isn't it? Poor old lady! Poor you, Dad!"

Oscar rolled his eyes in frustration but he looked brighter than he had done for a while. Relief was a powerful emotion. Ice's father looked hopeful, too, though still frazzled and unkempt – his normal appearance these days.

"You've eaten." It was more of a statement than a question. "Drink?"

Ice nodded the untruth about the food and accepted the cup of tea offered. She knew it was time to unburden herself to her dad. She would watch him closely for his reaction, though. She was still disturbed by the feeling of dishonesty during their previous conversation but she felt compelled to let him know about the files she had found, and about where she had taken them. Oscar also needed to hear it; he'd done the detective work, after all. She turned to her little brother.

"Have you told Dad about the computer?"

Oscar glared at her, crossly. She had expected him to keep the secret and now she was completely putting him on the spot. Ice quickly carried on, covering Oscar's indignant silence. Their father looked from one to the other and raised his eyebrows in anticipation of whatever it was they had to share.

"What?" he asked impatiently.

"Dad, there are some things we've found out that you need to know about," she said, and then, between her and Oscar, they filled him in on all the different parts of the story: the computer files; the emails; the connection with his boss and with Mr Bennett. Ice also told him about Anna King and the video and her intention to go to the police. Oscar reiterated how he had been certain when the police came, that his mother was fine. At least up until her last email. That there was another explanation. Even when the police had found the body he was sure it wasn't hers – she was alive somewhere. Throughout this, their father listened without speaking until they had pretty much ground to a halt and there was a silence. Ice broke it again.

"I know you told me that the drilling operation was totally safe, Dad, but that can't be right can it? Mum doesn't think so, does she? They're causing problems. She is pretty sure of it and so are a lot of people, here. Maybe the protestors are right. The stuff that's been going on… well it's a bit too much of a coincidence, isn't it? What if something has happened to her and it's all to do with this. Dad, we have to find her!" She finally really had run out of steam and she waited for his response.

Her dad said nothing for a moment. He pursed his lips and took in a breath, letting it out in a slow huff. He rubbed the stubble on his chin, pulled at his lower lip with his thumb and index finger. The children could see that his hands were trembling and he took another unsteady sip of his tea before finally uttering a single, "OK". They waited for more. He nodded slowly and repeated it, "OK, I can see that you've been digging into things that don't really concern you. You're just children, for goodness' sake! But... if what you've told me is true, we need to act quickly. What I don't understand is why you chose to go to a stranger rather than talk to me straight away." Ice avoided his glance. She did not want to tell him that she had not trusted him. She still did not think he was being utterly candid with them, even now. He was holding something back, but at least he wasn't very angry. What she felt from him was a combination of hope and fear. It would do to give him a half-truth for now and wait until she could understand what exactly it was that he was keeping from her.

"I'm sorry, Dad. I knew what you thought about the protestors though and I didn't want to make you angry. I just wanted to talk to somebody who wasn't involved – I couldn't leave it and Daniel gave me the chance there and then. Maybe I should have told you straight away. What are we going to do? How do we find mum? Where do we look? What could have happened?"

"The police are still following up the missing report but their resources are stretched. I need to think of a way of tracing her movements, Ice. Is she still in the States? Why was her ID at the site? Why would she be back in the UK early without telling us? Then I'm going to look at those files, so could you show me, please? I'll have to contact your friend's mother – this Mrs King – and see what she intends to do. Then you're going to try get some sleep. There's not much we can do now. The rest of it can wait until morning and it probably doesn't need you two to do any more sleuthing or building of conspiracy theories. Leave this to the adults, now, please."

"But what about Mum? What if she…" Oscar interjected.

"Like I said, Oscar, leave this to me, now. If there's anything that I need to tell you, I'll tell you."

Unusually, Ice found it hard to detect whether there was any deception or not in her father's reaction. Maybe he had genuinely accepted what they had told him; she had sensed neither truth nor lies about what he had said he was going to do, but only had that lingering feeling of disquiet whenever the topic of their mother came up. He always cut that conversation short somehow and she constantly had the impression that there was more he could have said.

Despite this uneasiness, it was a massive relief to have shared the information and the two children were very ready to show their father the documents they had found. Oscar went through the events again, explaining about the 'Magic Kitten' stories and pointing out how the old system worked with hidden files. Their dad let him rabbit on until finally he told the two children to leave him. It was a couple of hours before he was finished and Ice could have her room back.

Of course, sleep did not come easily when Ice did eventually get to bed. Though her thoughts felt just a little less tangled than they had before, she was kept awake by nagging images she could not erase: Joe's face as she had left him on the path; Nathan in his little, green beanie; her mother's ID card, muddy and creased but clearly still recognisable; visions of accident or disaster that Ice tried to dispel.

She must have eventually dropped off because at some point, Buddy had crept into her room without her knowing.

From her fitful sleep, she became aware of a low growl and was then brought to full consciousness by his distinctive boxer bark. On opening her eyes, she was confronted by two luminous almond shapes right in her line of vision. Ice froze. The creature was centimetres from her face – so close that she could see that the glowing shapes were not eyes, after all. Above these were its real ones, like two pools of black oil through which it gazed on her with interest and urgency. As Ice stirred, the shadeling moved to the door and back. Outside, more were on the street below, barely visible in the gloom. She was conscious that Buddy was still growling but she did not want to wake her brother and father and she tapped the dog quickly on the neck – his signal to stop.

"Come!" Ice said. She was certain she had to follow the shadeling, but she wasn't sure why. Buddy would be a welcome companion.

The weather was closing in again. Ice changed quickly into outside clothes and grabbed her thick socks for her wellies, which were by the back door. In the distance, there was the rumble of thunder. It was madness to be going out on a night like this and if she had thought about it rationally, she would have lost her nerve. But there was nothing rational about the compulsion she felt to follow the shadelings. As she slipped out, torch in hand and Buddy by her side, a tremendous explosion of light and sound told her the lightning was very close, but it was too late now. She was going.

The shadeling, appearing satisfied that Ice had understood its intention, now slipped along in front of them both, taking them on a route down the road and to the water's edge. This was the river which had completely burst its banks and was stretched across fields and the park on both sides. The shadeling continued, seemingly unaffected by the water, though Buddy, fresh off the leash, was delighted to splash through it. Ice was less enthusiastic. She could see the way the shadeling wanted her to go but wasn't keen for the water to over-top her boots. She tried to hug the higher parts of the bank, near the brick backs of the riverside houses, but the water was already a foot up the walls and though she made her way cautiously across the submerged bank, she could feel the cold liquid soaking into her socks. She need not have bothered trying to keep dry; as they all reached the metal steps up to the canal aqueduct, they were brilliantly illuminated by another intense flash of lightning and then the downpour began, soaking her completely within seconds.

Ice squelched her way up, clinging to the rail with one hand and holding the torch in the other. She was now in little doubt as to where the creature was taking her and no longer needed to keep it in view. At the top of the steps, she turned left along the canal towards the field of the Twelve Brothers and then followed the dog and the shadeling along the towpath and through the gate. It was eerie in the dark and the storm. She was glad of Buddy's earthy presence

The twelve stones did not look the way she had visualised them the last time she had visited the field. Now there was no imagined, prehistoric ceremony in the dying light of the day. The stones were barely visible, even though she was shining the torch through the sheets of rain. In that feeble beam, she could just make out that Buddy had stopped. He gave a couple of short barks and with his haunches lowered, began his trademark stalk towards something Ice could not see. As she took a step to follow him, many things happened at once. The entire scene was abruptly illuminated by another bolt of lightning, striking the tallest of the wet rocks. In that moment, Ice saw the familiar small figure of Nathan sail through the air, flung by the force of the electricity into the middle of the circle. Total darkness followed the flash. Although she was desperate to call out and run towards where Nathan had landed, she was rooted to the spot, unable to see clearly, nor utter a sound. Through the ringing in her ears, she could hear Buddy's frantic barking. There was the illusion that someone was calling her name just as it was drowned out by a rumbling crescendo from deep below and the ground heaved like a rolling wave. For a moment it was impossible for Ice to tell whether she had fallen to meet it or whether it had risen to smack her in the face. She could see nothing, but had the taste of wet dirt and grass and blood in her mouth, and she could still hear the horrific sounds of the earth tearing. She had no breath to scream and scrabbled frantically at the ground as it surged upwards, cutting her off from where Nathan had fallen. The rain had made the surface slick with mud, however, and there was nothing to stop her sliding backwards down the sloping earth into the gaping pit which had opened behind her. Ice fell from the storm and the wet and the darkness above, into the torn earth and the deeper darkness below.

In wildlife documentaries, there had always seemed to be that moment when a prey animal had stopped trying to struggle and accepted its fate. Ice had often wondered if it was the same for humans – if, at the moment that death was certain, fear became irrelevant. She certainly found herself no longer struggling to survive; she had lost all idea of which way up she was and there was no sense of where her limbs were. Enclosed spaces had always been a source of terror, but now Ice felt no panic – just a strong sense that she no longer had any control over any part of herself. She wondered if she were being crushed by the weight of earth above and whether this feeling that she was not really in her own body was part of a final madness. A delirium. Perhaps she was about to die. Ice could feel no distinction between herself and the rock. It was as though her body was sinking deep into it, dissolving through it while the earthquake shook out its fury way above her. This was like the shadelings, she thought to herself.

The delirium, if that's what it was, became more pronounced. Brief flashes of luminous yellowish green began to coalesce into the recognisable light patches of the shadelings. Gradually, Ice could see them altogether, swarming through the rock and gathering around her like curious children, and she knew without a doubt that this was their natural home. As if to confirm that thought, scenes began to unfold before her like a story. Ice was witnessing events as they had happened a long time ago. The shadelings were numerous and everything they needed to survive was far down in the earth. They flowed through the spaces in the rock where no spaces could even be seen. Sometimes they popped up through the surface and back down in the way she had noticed when she was last at the stones. They were curious about us but did not often involve themselves with the behaviour of the humans who lived in that other, solid world. Who knew how long they had inhabited this place and what organic life they had witnessed flourish and die out in their time? For millennia it seemed a near perfect existence.

But then there was a change. A shocking, panic-ridden change that made Ice's blood run cold again. A brutal intrusion came in the form of drills and chemicals, cracking the rocks apart and sucking out their source of energy, poisoning the earth and causing it to shudder and quake. This had driven them out of their own realm and forced them up to the surface. It was why Ice had seen so many in the real world lately. In the old tales, the shadelings may well have been the harbingers of doom, forewarning of earthquakes, plagues and other disasters, but this time, it was no natural disaster. Humans were entirely to blame. Stupidity or carelessness with our own world was having a catastrophic effect that threatened everything. It was interesting how people quickly accepted things as the new normal. Ice felt embarrassed that she had been so wrapped up in learning about the ancient past, she had closed her mind to what was going on in the present. She was sure that the chaotic weather and the earthquakes had been brought about by the actions of people. The shadelings were simply the victims trying to communicate with the few who could see them: the frightened man with the coat of badges; herself; a matter-of-fact young autistic boy... The thought brought Nathan's image to her mind and Ice could see him right at that moment. It was a confused jumble of pictures, though. The boy and the dog, tumbling together as the earth roiled and made to swallow them. Afterwards, not falling but being swept, carried along by unseen, familiar, dark forms, through the rock – not like Ice was, mysteriously in the fabric itself, but through real tunnels beneath the old stones, under the ground and into a buried chamber inside a hill. Mort's Hill.

Suddenly, she had the sensation of being grabbed by the wrist and there was a painful wrenching of her shoulder as sensation flooded back. Someone was calling her name. There was fear and desperation in the sound and Ice became aware of two skinny arms that had reached for her, gripping fiercely and pulling, fighting against the still writhing earth. She felt a sickening crack and heard a cry of pain, though she did not know if it was hers or another's. Instantly fighting for her life again, Ice kicked her legs, bracing them against anything solid below and pushing herself up, until she could feel the cold rain and the rush of air against her face. She rolled free and lay flat out in the mud while the tremors continued and then faded to nothing. From above, unabated, the rain streamed down over her and the boy lying next to her.

"I couldn't save him." Joe was sobbing in pain and grief and frustration. "They've gone. It took them so quickly – there was nothing I could do!"

Ice dug her phone out of her pocket, pressed the emergency dial button and then lost consciousness.

Chapter 14
Hospital

When Ice next opened her eyes, there were too many people around her. It took her a moment to realise that she must have been found and transported to hospital, though it was disconcerting that she had no memory of any of it. When she tried to sit up, she was thwarted by an excruciating pain in her left shoulder and she noticed that it was strapped up with her arm in a sling. Her soaking clothes were nowhere to be seen – she was wearing a hideous hospital robe.

"It's OK," someone (a nurse or a doctor?) said. It was a female voice. "You've had a nasty wrench, but there's no permanent damage. Your shoulder will feel sore for a while and you've got just a few cuts and bruises. Your friend was lucky, too. His arm is broken in three places, but we've managed to set it and it should mend well enough. I'm giving you the all clear to check out. There's no obvious head injury, but you were 'out of it' for a while, so…" she turned to Ice's father, "You'll need monitoring at home." But now, I'd very much like it if all these people could let me have this corridor back as soon as possible. The casualties are still coming in." With that, she left them to themselves.

"Did she mean Joe, when she said 'your friend'?" Ice thought, remembering the sight of the boy spread-eagled next to her on the shattered ground. Where was he? It took effort to concentrate and think about the other people around her. The hospital looked like it had withstood the earthquake well. She could see no sign of damage, but the corridor was full of people lying on beds or sitting on plastic chairs nursing minor injuries and there was some bustle as hospital personnel tried to deal with them all. Here was her dad, now helping her to sit up and here, Oscar, his face showing unusual levels of excitement. His eyes had a wide, slightly unhinged look and he was almost hopping up and down. There was Nathan's mum – and Mr Bennett.

"You!" Ice said, raising her voice at the man. The pain had made her careless. "This is all your fault! And yours!" She turned on her father, too. "You've done this with your stupid machines and your chemicals and your pumps and your drills!"

Nathan's father looked furious. He frowned and opened his mouth as if to say something but closed it again and did not reply and Ice knew he had understood her completely. Her father seemed unbothered by her accusation. His face was more relaxed than she had seen it in a long time. Did he actually smile? Mrs Bennett was standing away from her husband, alone. She held her arms folded across her middle, hands clenched on either side. Next to her were the two police officers they had met before. Ice had to repress the urge to laugh out loud. Perhaps it was the endorphins from the pain. She'd heard they could make you light-headed. Or maybe it was being the unwanted centre of attention, but the whole scene looked to her like a silly set-piece from an old hospital movie. All it needed now was a handsome, white-coated doctor to shoo everyone out, telling them that the patient needed to rest. Ice bit her lip and closed her eyes.

Mrs Bennett spoke quietly and with obvious effort to keep her voice steady. "Ice – what happened to Nathan? Did you see him? The police have looked for him where you were found – Joe told them that he was there and you both saw him. Was he… did he…" She couldn't maintain the control as her voice broke and she started to cry.

"No!" Ice exclaimed. She looked up at the skylight above her. The glimmer of morning was breaking through as the clouds of last night's storm drifted off into grey patches. The early stillness outside did not give away the turmoil of the night. "He's not… I mean Nathan went under… I know where to find him. I can show you! You have to let me get dressed and out of here to take you there now!"

Maybe this was not what they were expecting to hear. Ice detected a range of uncomfortable reactions and then her father cut in. "Ice – it's OK. You've been through a lot and you're supposed to be careful, now. I know you want to help but the police have searched that whole area." He dropped his voice until it was almost inaudible. "I think Nathan's not coming back. I'm so sorry. The boy, Joe, told us that he saw them – Nathan and Buddy – disappear into a rift. Stones toppled. The whole place is unrecognisable. It'll take them weeks to dig down and find them… their bodies… Also, Ice… there's…" he paused without finishing what he was going to say and Ice noticed him give Oscar a meaningful look.

Mr Bennett turned away. He pressed his fingers against his forehead as though trying to massage away a bad headache and then stopped, his hands still covering his face, and stood still as though he had simply run out of power.

Ice struggled up. She felt a rising sense of urgency and she needed at least one of these adults to pay attention to what she was saying. They all seemed to have different plans.

"Dad, we need to go. Now! Mrs Bennett, listen to me. I know where Nathan is. You must trust me. I can take you there but we need to hurry!"

Oscar was suddenly at her side.

"Here," he said. "They're not completely dry – but they're better than they were!" He held out an orange shopping bag that contained her clothes and Ice was supremely grateful to her little brother.

"Can you at least let my sister get dressed in private?" he said to the group, and they appeared to gather their wits and agree to leave her in peace, moving down the corridor.

"Wait!" Ice called. She addressed PC Owens. "Joe didn't see everything I did. I know what happened. Can you come? I think we'll need you to send for help. And you, Mrs Bennet. Wait for us – follow us. Dad – can you take us there in your car?"

"Ice, I don't really know what this is all about, nor what good it'll do, but you're obviously set on something. I know you well enough to be sure you won't let up once you get an idea in your head – so, yes. I will try to take you to the stones… but first…"

"No, Dad! Not the stones. He's not there, but I know where he is. I think… I'm sure Nathan and Buddy are there."

Her dad seemed disengaged from what she was saying. It wasn't as though he wasn't taking her seriously or he didn't believe her – it was like he was only half listening to her.

Oscar couldn't take it any longer.

"Ice! We need to show you something!" he cut in. He looked on the verge of giggling.

It was a struggle to get dressed with the effective use of only one arm and trying to be discreet in the corridor. With some wriggling and squirming, she managed to get her jeans on under the hospital gown. Then she needed Oscar's help but it was awkward – he was turning away to give her privacy, while at the same time trying to help her to remove the gown and to put on her own top, one sleeve hanging loosely over her strapped arm. By the end, she was exhausted and tears of pain threatened to give away her discomfort. However, between them they managed to get her dressed and she let Oscar help her on with her wellies before she slid off the trolley to stand up.

"Come on!" her brother insisted, dragging her along by her good arm. Ice was still dazed and let Oscar and her dad lead her along the busy corridors of the hospital to a quieter ward. This was a small room with only four hospital beds, all occupied. In one, an elderly lady was sitting propped against the cushions while she watched the television that was suspended on the opposite wall. It was muted and the sub-titles were scrolling across the screen so as not to disturb the other patients. It took Ice a moment to realise that one of them was staring straight at her and smiling. Her shoulder-length, dark hair had been partly shaven, revealing a stitched head-wound. Both eyes were surrounded by purplish, yellowing bruising, but she was still unmistakably recognisable.

"Mum!" Ice said. "You look like a punk! Great hairstyle! What happened? Where have you been?" Then she moved quickly to the bedside and mother and daughter gave each other a rather awkward and careful embrace, both conscious that the other was injured.

"It's a long story," her mother replied. "I'm so sorry I worried you. My phone is a write-off. I couldn't contact you or anybody until just now. I'm fine. But what happened to you – your arm?"

Ice looked down at her sling and gave a sheepish laugh.

"Maybe we both have a story to tell," she said. "Thank goodness, you're OK. But Mum, what the hell?" By this time Oscar was bouncing up and down next to her, shouting "I told you, didn't I? I knew it." Ice's father had pulled up one of the chairs provided for hospital visitors.

"We'll try to explain everything," he said. "But maybe we should do this at home. Are you able to leave now?" He turned to his wife. She shook her head and pulled a face.

"They said overnight for observation and discharged tomorrow, hopefully," she replied.

Ice nodded. She wanted to go home now, with her mum. She wanted to lie down without the gripping pain in her shoulder, but she had not forgotten that people were waiting for her.

"We have to go, Mum," she said. "Buddy's missing. And my friend, Nathan. We're going to find them."

Chapter 15
Mort's Hill

"Where are we going?" Ice's father asked as he started up the engine. She had taken four painkillers in the car and was feeling light-headed but she leaned over and tapped in the letters for 'Mort's Hill' on the SatNav, hoping that the route it showed would still be drivable.

Oscar was uncharacteristically animated in the back, jiggling up and down in his seat and for once, looking out and not down at his phone screen. Though there were signs of the disturbance that had happened in the night, nothing resembled what Ice had experienced at the stones. Their route through the Warwickshire countryside was uninterrupted, if a little slow behind drivers who were being overly cautious. It did mean that the police had no trouble keeping up. PC Owens had been sceptical but Ice was glad that she had decided to follow. It was likely that Mrs Bennett had been persuasive. The journey may only have been five miles or so, but it was through some meandering country roads that, combined with the pain and the effect of the painkillers, made it almost intolerable for Ice. However, she was acutely aware that though she thought she knew where Nathan and Buddy were because she had seen them taken there, she did not know *how* they were. The determination to find them now, kept her from giving in to fatigue and nausea.

Their father turned off on to a gritty track and then came to a stop where the SatNav announced that they had reached their destination. They were at the foot of Mort's Hill. It was an open, scrubby area that gave way to gorse and low tangles of brambles, before rising into a grassy lump on the landscape. Ice stared at the hill and wondered what on earth she was supposed to do next. In the tumultuous vision of the night before, she had pictured Nathan and Buddy, deep inside this feature, safe in a hollow cavity. Now it looked like it was nonsense. The sides of the hill were completely unbroken by any hint of a cave or entrance to the interior. With a rush of brakes on shingle, the police car drew up beside them. Both officers got out on to the path and Ice saw that Mr and Mrs Bennett had accompanied them in the back. Feeling woozy and disorientated, Ice tried to gather her thoughts; the adults would want to know why she had brought them here, and it was difficult to think of a way to explain it or convince them she wasn't crazy.

"Nathan is in there," Ice said, pointing at the mound. All except Oscar reacted with looks of astonishment or dismay, even anger, but she pressed on. "I know it sounds ridiculous, but you have to get in there somehow. There's a cave or something inside." She was feeling desperate and quite ill.

"This isn't funny," Owens said, looking furious. "Wasting police time is an offence! How could they possibly be in there?" She took Mrs Bennett's arm and began to steer her back towards the car. "I'm so sorry, Mrs Bennett. I must apologise for this – I thought she had some real information on his whereabouts."

Mrs Bennett, however, shook off the guidance and approached Ice. "What do you mean, Ice? Why do you think he's in there?"

Ice could not say that she had 'seen' them carried deep underground from the stones to the hill – saved by the shadelings and deposited safe away from the earthquake and the falling rocks. Despite herself, she could feel the hot threat of tears and she began to make her way through the undergrowth to the hillside, desperately looking for some kind of crack that would give away the inner chamber.

"It must be here! We've all got to try to find it!" Ice called. "Help me find an entrance or something."

Owens watched. Her expression betrayed her annoyance at what she thought was an elaborate hoax. The young officer stood at her side. He looked undecided as to whether he should share her disapproval or join in the crazy search. But Oscar, and then her father and Mrs Bennett and then even Mr Bennett began to look, none of them certain of what she was telling them, but all willing it not to be a cruel waste of their time. They tramped through the wiry stalks of the brambles and scrutinised the surface, some kneeling to part the grass, others pulling away small boulders that might have concealed an entrance. The more they looked, the more it seemed a fantasy. With the first flush of determination now fading, Ice was struggling. Her shoulder was aching and she was nearly useless, scrabbling one-handed at the rocky ground that was obstinately solid beneath the wet outer later. Losing the will to continue, she sagged against the slope and lay her head on the rough earth. For a while she stayed there, too exhausted to move, while the others maintained their search with decreasing hope. Ice closed her eyes. Her head felt weighty and she could sense each texture on her cheek as she pressed it against the hill – the smooth roundness of small pebbles and the damp edges of the blades of grass. Her tiredness made it all rather comfortable, and the earthy smell began to act like a drug, drawing her in to sleep. She drifted, only aware now, of the sounds of the others. Owens was talking on her phone – there was a crackled reply. Close by, a blackbird broke into a melodious song – probably glad to have some dry weather after all the rain. Somewhere, far away, a dog barked. Ice sat up, startled by her recognition of the sound. Buddy! That was Buddy's bark! She pressed her ear back to the ground and there it was again, Buddy's unmistakable tones announcing his presence right inside the hill!

"Here!" she called, wide awake now. "They're in here. Listen!"

Chapter 16
Out of the Dark

Sometimes the adults did what they were supposed to do. The digger was available and arrived within the hour. Mrs Bennett had her ear pressed to the ground for pretty much the whole time, shouting Nathan's name but with no response apart from Buddy's distant barks. The digging passed like a dream for Ice, who watched it from the front seat of the car, struggling to stay awake and to cope with the swimming sensation in her head. The others had stayed outside and now stood in a loose group, silently observing the rhythm of the machine. It must have been fascinating for Oscar, Ice thought to herself as the yellow bucket sunk its teeth effortlessly into the soil and was swung round in a neat curve to deposit each load to the side. A mound of fresh earth built quickly. At one point the operator of the excavator stopped it and jumped down, walking round to the front to inspect the progress. Ice could see some words pass between him and the adults in the group. Mrs Bennett said something and pointed in Ice's direction and then down at the newly created trench.

The man shrugged and resumed his digging in the same place. Ice leaned her head against the side window and closed her eyes, feeling guilty that she longed for bed when Buddy and Nathan were so far from theirs. She was aware that she must have begun to drift, when she was suddenly jerked back to wakefulness by a shout of success from the operator. She saw, miraculously, the collapse of rock and soil which revealed a dark entrance to the hill. Ice leaned forward over the steering wheel and observed as the adults approached the hole; they were held back by the police officers who were communicating with some distant superior on their walkie-talkies. The young male police officer was gesturing to the group and then he unclipped his torch, crouched down and disappeared into the opening. Her heart was pounding uncomfortably now – she had been right about the hill! It had to be true – Nathan would be there, surely. Ice clambered with some effort out of the car and half ran, half limped over to the others.

There was an air of renewed hope among the group now, though they all looked grubby and tired. Ice could sense a range of different attitudes towards her as she joined them. Owens was still communicating by walkie-talkie – perhaps with the policeman in the tunnel – but Ice could see the doubtful glance she gave her as she arrived. Oscar was wide-eyed and grinning at her. He pointed at the digger and then the hole and made an exaggerated 'O' with his mouth. She accepted a brief hug from her dad and nodded in response to his asking if she was OK. Nathan's dad avoided looking at her but Mrs Bennett, she thought, was full of anticipation and terrified at the same time. It was often like this, Ice thought – hope of success made people scared of failure. What if they had come this far and it was all for nothing? The longer they waited, the more their excitement turned to anxiety. This was compounded by news from Owens that she could no longer make contact with her colleague underground.

"He shouldn't have gone in by himself!" she said. "I told him backup was coming but he insisted we shouldn't wait! He doesn't have the right gear – not even a hard hat – and we still don't know for certain that there's any point in looking in there! This is going to go on my report – I didn't agree to this at all."

"He made a decision," said Mrs Bennett. "Maybe it was not quite protocol, but it's my son's life – I'm grateful to him! Do you see any backup? There isn't any. How long were we supposed to wait for it? My son could be in danger in there. Now that he's gone in, we need to be patient and let your colleague do this."

It was hard to be patient, though. The policewoman paced alongside the digger. She had refused to let the operator return it to the depot and he was now sitting smoking in the cab. Every now and then she stood by the tunnel entrance and shone her torch with futility into the blackness. Ice and the others eventually grew tired of waiting on their feet and sat. It was taking far too long.

"Oh, Buddy!" she heard Oscar say and her heart lurched, seeing in her mind's eye his lifeless form brought to the surface. But it was only a brief moment of doubt and she was wrong. There was her very real, very alive dog emerging unscathed and apparently undaunted by his night underground. He wriggled and sniffed his way around the entire party, going from one to the other in excited circles until she finally grabbed him by his collar and buried her face in the thick scruff of his neck, sharing him with Oscar who was trying to hug him, and blissfully breathing in his warm biscuit odour which was now mingled with the smell of damp earth. Even though Ice had tried to cling on to the feeling of certainty about the chamber in the hill, Buddy's arrival was still incredible. He had broken the apprehensive mood of the group but all eyes now turned eagerly back to the tunnel. They waited. Nobody came.

Buddy was trying to pull Ice back towards the hill but she had a tight hold of his collar. He barked in frustration and at that moment the policeman came into view, blinking in the light. He was holding in his arms what looked like a dishevelled bundle of dirty clothes. Mrs Bennett gave a cry of recognition and then Ice could see two small muddy legs, one shoe missing, and she heard a familiar, serious and deep little voice relating in a long stream of detail, the events as they had happened. Mrs Bennett was there immediately as the policeman released hold of the child and passed him into her arms. It was funny to see Nathan's small hands still gesticulating over his mother's shoulder, as he continued his lengthy explanation while she held him tightly. When Nathan's father wrapped them both in his embrace, his mother made no attempt to resist but continued to hug her child to herself as though to physically confirm the wonderful truth of his discovery, safe and alive. Nathan was still talking when Mrs Bennett brought him over to Ice.

"And basically," he said and then paused as he recognised her, "Well you are that new girl at my school and you were there in the old stones and those things were happening that were dangerous and I didn't like the thunder. I was putting my hands over my ears. It was too loud. Basically, the creakers didn't like the machines in the ground and they showed me where to go to the stones but then the ground was moving like this and they were going to fall and the lightning was too bright. I didn't like it." He pointed at Buddy and continued. "That is a good dog and we were together in that dark hill and I couldn't see anything but that dog stayed there and I could touch him so I wasn't scared and the creakers put us in because it was safe but I didn't know how long we were meant to stay. Everywhere was black and there was nothing to eat and then that dog barked for a long time and it was noisy. Well, basically, I wanted to get out then and we heard that digger." Nathan waved his arms towards the yellow machine.

Nathan's incongruously dry monologue forced a weary smile from Ice, "His name's Buddy," she said. "I'm glad you looked after each other!"

"You are making a wet face," Nathan said, and he reached out and rubbed Ice's cheek with his index finger, making a muddy trail in her warm tears that were finally flowing, unchecked.

Mrs Bennett did not need to say anything; she simply leant down towards Ice and placed her forehead to hers in a wordless gesture of thanks, before moving off to the police car which was waiting to take them to the hospital where Nathan could be checked before going home. Mr Bennett lingered for a moment.

"I owe you a great debt of gratitude," he muttered awkwardly, looking down quickly so as not to meet Ice's gaze. He sighed and there was a pause. Ice's father and Oscar stood by her side, Buddy now sitting on her feet, all watching Mr Bennett, nobody knowing quite how to respond.

"I'm… um… thank you and sorry," he said briefly and walked quickly away to join his wife in the police car.

"Come," said Mr Cooper, "It's time we got home. Ice, I don't know how you knew about these astonishing things, but that little boy is safe because of you. You've done your bit for today, I think."

They were intercepted on the way to their car by Owens who said, "I should make an apology to you, Ice. I don't claim to understand anything of this and I'll need to write a report. I'm not sure how I'm going to explain it all. I will need your statement. Someone will be in touch in a couple of days."

Ice's father ignored the policewoman and steered his children towards the car.

"Perhaps you can tell me about it later," he whispered, "when you've had some rest – but for now we should get you to bed. You look like you're about to drop."

"You are looking a bit grey," chimed in her younger brother. "You and mum should be in a zombie film together – you don't need any makeup!" Ice pulled a disdainful face at him, but she knew what he was doing. Teasing her right now was his way of bringing some normality to the extraordinary events they had been experiencing. She thought of having her mother home. She thought of her bed and nothing seemed more appealing. Though she had been running on adrenaline and sheer determination over the past ten hours or so, the discovery of Nathan had meant that she could give in to the fatigue that was overwhelming her. Ice nodded her assent to her dad and was asleep in the back of the car long before they reached the house; this time she didn't even notice the long winding journey that would normally make her feel sick.

Chapter 17
Confessions

It was dark again when Ice finally woke. She didn't know how long she had been asleep, but the pain in her shoulder had forced her to consciousness and she found she was desperately thirsty and needed to pee. She flicked on her phone to see that it said 02:36. She had slept since they had arrived home, over twelve hours ago! Ice, grateful that it was a Saturday, rolled clumsily out of bed and shuffled to the bathroom where she found the painkillers and took one. It was very quiet. She listened intently for any of the sounds that had punctuated the last few days – the creaking of the shadelings, the trickle of water in the guttering, the deep rumble of a pending quake – but they were all absent. All good, Ice thought, as she made her way back to bed.

"Ice, is that you?" She heard her father's hushed voice. "Are you awake?"

Ice did not answer, but instead sought him out in the kitchen, where she found him sitting alone, surrounded by papers, at the table, Buddy snoring gently in the corner.

"How are you?" her dad queried. "Are you OK to talk, or do you need to get back to bed?"

"I'm OK," she said, rubbing her shoulder. "A bit sore, but not too tired." She was tired, really, and going back to sleep would have been nice, but she knew that she wouldn't be able to now. She'd be thinking about what it was that her father wanted to say to her – he had a lot of explaining to do – so she sat down opposite him and waited for him to speak.

"I hadn't really registered how much you've grown up," he said, still looking down at the papers in front of him. "At first, I thought I was protecting you and Oscar, but now I can

112

see that keeping you out of it meant keeping you at arm's length – creating distance. It wasn't what I wanted. I wasn't trying to lie to you, Ice."

He looked up at her and she wondered if she was meant to respond. Not 'trying to lie' meant nothing. He had lied. Or at least, he hadn't told her the truth. She wasn't sure where he was going with this talk so she let the silence linger until he was forced to continue.

"You asked me before about Mum and I wasn't entirely honest."

"I know," Ice replied. Her dad glanced at her sharply but then pulled a wry expression and continued.

"I think I probably knew that you knew," he said. "You take after her quite a lot. Oh I know you look more like me, but she could always tell things about people that I couldn't see. I'm just an engineer, after all. Machines are my thing. Give me a problem with a drill pipe or a technical issue and I'm great. With people, less so – as you and poor old Oscar are fully aware, I suppose!" He seemed to be delaying getting to the point, but Ice didn't want to put him off so she just nodded and waited.

"That was the thing that kicked it all off. Your mother, I mean. She has far more to do with the people in the company and she began to get the sense that there were things not right – just a feeling at first. I didn't take it seriously enough, I suppose. I didn't want to believe her. I tried to convince myself that it was just anti-fracking propaganda – the kind of stuff we'd been dealing with for ages – and, you know, I had a job to do. But your mum didn't let up. We got into a massive fight about it. She said that she had evidence that the company was covering up the risks involved – faking reports about the environmental impact – accidentally 'misplacing' vital documents. At first, I refused to listen. Then I began to worry – I didn't want her to take it on. These people were our bosses. Whistle-blowing is a dangerous business. It never ends well for the person, nor their family. I told her to think of our future – of you two."

It was odd. Part of her felt her father's story was unreal – the stuff of fiction – a television drama, perhaps, but Ice could also see that it made complete sense. It was possibly the least implausible thing that she had learned about in the past few days. She also simultaneously saw the point of view of both parents. Although Ice got her father's predicament entirely, she could understand exactly how her mother must have been feeling. She knew she had this similarity with her – the inability to let injustice go unhindered. If people were doing something bad, it was hard to ignore it and do nothing. What Ice found hard to forgive, though, was that her dad had kept her in the dark. She frowned.

"Dad... why did you not tell me this when I asked you? I thought you were hiding things from me. It was horrible! I was beginning to imagine you were involved with the bad stuff! What happened to Mum? Why are you still working for that awful company?"

"It was adult business," he replied, and it was unclear which question he was answering – perhaps all three. "I mean I think I was protecting you and Oscar. I didn't lie totally about your mum. We were really angry with each other. We weren't speaking or communicating. I had this horrible inkling she might have decided to do something dangerous and I was furious. I assumed she was with me, too. I tried to put it from my mind and carry on as normal with the move and the job, but I think you must have noticed I wasn't quite myself. When you told me that you hadn't heard from her either, I began to panic but I was still trying to not show it. If she was in danger, it was my fault – she couldn't persuade me to take on the company. It all became much more serious than I expected and I just thought, I hoped, she'd get in touch soon. When that ID was found, I was confused and – I'm not too proud to admit it – a little terrified. I didn't know what to do. Going to identify that body was the worst moment in my life. Then you and Oscar uncovered her files and gave them to Mrs King and I realised I couldn't bury my head in the sand any longer. She wasn't responding to any texts or phone calls but that evening I did some research of my own. Did you know you can download an app that will track someone's phone, even if it's not working? You can get these on the dark web – ones that don't even need to have the other phone – just the number. The one I found told me that your mum's phone was off, but it gave me her last known location. I couldn't believe it! What was she thinking? She was on the closed site. What was she doing there? Snooping? Looking for evidence. What did she expect to find? Why had there been no contact from her. It was mad. This isn't the movies, for goodness' sake!"

Ice felt that it was very much like the movies, but she let him go on.

"Apparently, she had finished work early in Dallas and had decided to join us straight away. A 'surprise' she told me, though I suspect our big fight also had something to do with why she didn't let me know. She caught the plane back Monday. The day you were in trouble. She got here early Tuesday morning. And this is where it gets silly, Ice. It's like a plot in a disaster film. Instead of coming straight home, your mum decides to go to the local site. She said that she wanted photographs of hard copies of documents at the site office and to email them to herself. The ones which are needed before the drilling starts. She was sure they'd either be faked or would show that we shouldn't be drilling there. Those were the ones on the email that you and Oscar found. She sent them straight from the site computer. Our 'office' is little more than a steel box on site. You know – one of those huts they put up, like the temporary classrooms you had in your last school. It's all one building with a main room, a single door and a toilet cubicle. And that was the day we went up to the site to lock it down because of the floods."

Ice opened her eyes wide at this information, almost predicting what was coming next. It was a mad story, but she didn't want to interrupt him now that he was in full flow. She nodded, silently.

"She told me that she heard us talking and doing our lock up, and panicked, hiding in the toilet cubicle. How ridiculous is that, Ice? She was actually there when I was shutting everything down.

He sighed and rolled his eyes. Ice pulled up a stool by the table and prompted him to continue.

"She doesn't know when she lost her ID but it must have been at some time when she was outside. Apparently, she had put it on in case anybody saw her at the site and she had to try to explain herself. Clearly it got pulled off somehow and washed away by the floodwaters. It was pretty treacherous up there. She doesn't remember much after that, apart from trying the door handle and finding herself locked in the hut. She can recall not being able to open the drawers on the desk and looking for a key, then giving up and thinking about climbing out of the only window. That must have been when the earthquake hit. You know, Ice, your mum was trapped in that building for two days. Nearly three!"

"What? Why didn't she get out of the window? What happened to her?" Ice asked, finally breaking her silence.

"Well I don't know exactly what happened and she can't remember because she was knocked unconscious. I think I've figured it out though. After I saw the information from the tracking app, I went straight out and back to the site. You and Oscar were both already in bed. Or at least I thought so! I didn't like leaving you without telling you anything, but it seemed better than disturbing you and getting you all worried, or dragging you both out to the site. Anyway, when I got there, the weather was horrendous."

Ice knew this. She had been out in it herself, that night.

"I had to be really careful. The holes we had drilled were hidden beneath the water and rivers of mud were flowing round the building. It was dark, but when I turned on the big lights, I saw immediately that one of the huge vehicles holding the plant equipment had been shifted by the earth tremor and had slid into the hut, impacting one wall and blocking the window."

Ice put her hand over her mouth. Her mother was fine now in hospital, but she could have been crushed to death and nobody would have known about it.

"I think she had fallen over backwards, hit her head on the desk and knocked herself out. I don't know how long she was unconscious, but by the time I got there, she had already tried hammering at the door with anything she could find, she said. Those metal walls are built to be secure though. People are not supposed to be able to break in. Or out, it would seem! Her phone was smashed."

"Poor Mum!" Ice said. "It must have been awful!" She thought about her mum trapped in the dark. It wasn't so different to what had happened to her, but she hadn't been alone for days. Her dad must have been taking her mum to hospital at about the time she was at the stone circle. No wonder he was there when she woke up after the big earthquake.

"With concussion, too!" he replied. "Thankfully, the hut had a water supply that was still working. And thankfully I still had my set of keys! When I unlocked the door, I found her curled up on the hard floor. I think she was quite pleased to see me!"

It was clear to Ice that her father was now being honest with her and in his relief, a little of his sense of humour was returning. She worked to keep her emotions in check. His words made the picture a lot clearer, but she wasn't ready to forgive him entirely. And there were a lot of unsolved issues. What were the chances of them being a proper family? Surely her mother couldn't keep working for that company, knowing what she knew. And what about her father? They seemed friendly at the hospital, but they had had a big disagreement over what to do. Would they be able to take on the company? Would they be out of work? Large companies seemed to have a way of getting what they wanted. If they couldn't stop it, the fracking would start up again after the floods – the damage would still be done. The shadelings, that had tried so hard to warn them in the only way they could, would still be destroyed and almost nobody would be any the wiser.

"Dad, do you at least agree with Mum now? You know that the earthquakes are caused by the fracking, don't you?" she ventured. "Those protesters were right, weren't they? It's not safe."

He shook his head and shrugged. "That's what she believes," he replied. "It looks like she – they – are right after all. Whatever the case, the drilling in Warwickshire has been halted for the foreseeable future. I hope there'll be a proper investigation. I think Mrs King is a bit of a crusader. She won't let this go. The police should be speaking to Mr Bennett and David Hunt. But my drill site is a disaster-zone. The earthquake and the floods have caused irreparable damage. It would take time to get it operational, even if we were permitted to do so."

It was a lot to take in, but for once her head was not spinning. Knowledge really did make all the difference and there were many things she now understood. The truth was liberating and had allowed tiredness to overwhelm her. She was very glad to not have school in the morning. It would be wise to try and get a bit more sleep before dawn, at any rate. Ice stood up and walked back to the kitchen door.

"Sorry, Ice," her father said.

She paused in the doorway and then nodded briefly before taking herself up the stairs to her bedroom.

She was half asleep when she became aware of a dim glow and opened her eyes to find a small group of the shadelings gathered in a semi-circle just a metre or so from the bed. They were almost like old friends now, she thought. It was strange to remember how intimidated she had been at first.

"What do you guys want, now?" she whispered in mock exasperation. "You're safe. They've stopped the machines and you can go back to doing whatever it is you normally do!" Of course, there was no answer from the small creatures – they were being unusually quiet. Instead, one of them approached her, sat catlike just in front of her face and pointed a small, clawed digit towards her. Cautiously, in turn, Ice reached out to touch it with the tip of her own finger. She laughed inwardly. Oscar would have liked to see this – it was just like the scene in 'ET'. She was slightly disappointed that, unlike the boy in the film, she wasn't suddenly miraculously free from pain, but she did have a strange sensation of simultaneous warmth and cold on her fingertip. There was no solid feeling from the small creature. Ice smiled.

"You're welcome," she said, "and thank you, too. You should be safe for a while. Is this 'Goodbye'? Or will I be seeing you again sometime…?"

Chapter 18
Amnesty

She might have gone to sleep after that because she had no recollection of the shadelings departing from her room. When she next opened her eyes, it was daylight, someone was knocking on the door and there was a commotion outside in the street.

Ice had seen footage on the news of the 'paparazzi' gathered outside people's houses and it took her only a moment to realise that this was what was happening to her own family. It was amazing how quickly information spread these days. The Net had made everything almost instantaneous. Their letter-box flipped open and someone called, "Ice, can you tell us how you knew where Nathan was? What happened to your mother? Is it true that the drilling site has been shut down because it was causing the earthquakes? Will the police be talking to the site manager? What about Councillor Bennett? Didn't he agree to the fracking operation?" She imagined that if they had had an old house phone like the ones in films, it would have been ringing off the hook. It was very intrusive – some of the journalists were even pressing cameras up against the front window trying to get a photograph.

Her father called the two children from the landing, told them to get dressed quickly so they could go out the back door and away from the house up the side alley while he distracted the invaders. This Oscar did. It took Ice a little longer, with her arm in a sling. Then they slipped out, only needing to break into a run as one of the photographers caught sight of them a little way down the road. Ice could see

Oscar staring at her aghast as they stumbled breathlessly into the supermarket and hid themselves in the aisles.

"It's alright," she said. "There's nobody following. I'm sure they'll lose interest very soon – when the next silly story comes along!"

"Is this a silly story?" Oscar asked, and Ice remembered that he had not been party to her father's conversation with her in the early hours of the morning. She didn't know how much her dad had told him at the hospital. Before answering his question, Ice took him by the hand and pulled him purposefully towards the door and out into the rare spring sunshine. He followed obediently across the road to the small, open square where they found an almost dry bench and she filled him in on all the gaps.

"Wow! That's all just ... wow!" he said, with a low whistle. "I thought I was right, but I was really right! Mum the detective?"

"Yes," she said.

She was not sure how long the pair of them sat there in the middle of Depton, silent with their own thoughts. The little square was a trap for the sun which they were both reluctant to leave – it had been such a rare occurrence to see things this brightly and feel its warmth recently. There was, however, something that Ice needed to do. Several somethings, in fact.

"Come," she said, getting up suddenly.

It was fortunate Depton was a compact town. Even so, they covered a lot of residential ground that morning. Ice had an air of determination. She had weathered storms. She'd faced floods and earthquakes. She'd rescued a boy and a dog and talked to supernatural creatures. She could manage a few social interactions! Nevertheless, it was still a comfort to have

Oscar's company. Daniel and his mother welcomed her warmly, when she arrived on their doorstep. They pressed her for details while she tried to express her gratitude. Here, she asked if Oscar could stay for a while away from the journalists and the photographers. Mrs King readily agreed – he and Daniel could swap app tips. Mrs King told her the next two addresses she needed, but she had to ask Daniel about the other. He wasn't completely sure. At Mia's, Ice managed to initiate a friendly embrace on the doorstep before being invited in to share her incredible story. Nathan's mother cried again but laughed and apologised when Ice yelped at being squeezed. Nathan told her that basically the creakers were happy and they had gone home.

***

The road was a familiar one – though very different from the last time she had seen it. Part the way home, and off to the left, she walked briskly up the narrow pavement, checking the house numbers as she went. She hoped her information was correct. Ice knocked and waited. There was the sound of a key in the lock and the door opened. A skinny, dark-haired boy stood in the doorway. It was odd to see him properly, pale still, the bright sunlight accentuating the dark rings under his eyes. Ice noticed the plaster cast on his arm and the surprised look on his face.

"Hello, Joe," she said.

ACKNOWLEDGEMENT

Many thanks to all the friends and family who beta read the versions of Ice Cooper and the Depton Shadelings and who gave me encouragement and critical feedback. I would also like to thank my Year 5 and 6 pupils for being my very first guinea-pigs (you know who you are) and JH in particular, who asked me what happened in the story when it was nothing more than a starter prompt. Thanks also to my editor, Kirsty Ridge, for thorough and essential work, helping me to knock it into shape.

ABOUT THE AUTHOR

J A Bowler

J A Bowler originates in Zimbabwe but now lives in Warwickshire and often draws on the local environment in story settings. Having taught primary aged children for the best part of three decades, the author is now a freelance writer and artist who also sometimes plays in bands on saxophones and bass guitar.

You can connect with me on:

Author site: https://jabowler.wordpress.com

Twitter: https://twitter.com/JBowler_author

Email: julietbowler@outlook.com